# The Devil's Vortex

## John Devlin

**aabspec books**

The Devil's Vortex.  ISBN 0-9527768-2-0

Published by Aabspec International Ltd., Ireland.
E-Mail: words@aabspec.com

Cover Design by Hugh O'Neill, Dublin, Ireland.
Printed by Litho Press & Co., Midleton, Cork, Ireland.

AABSPEC
NEW YORK · DUBLIN · DÜSSELDORF

I would like to express my appreciation to those who have assisted in various ways over the past few years to bring this story to publication. It was against a tide of some difficulty.

The first professional editor who expressed a view, said it would never be published in Britain or Ireland because of the political content. Another said she found it hard to believe the events described could happen. Perhaps everyone who reads this book will find something to upset them. But then it may also encourage those who do read it to reflect on some of the odder aspects of life, the things we don't often talk about.

I've really enjoyed writing this story. My wish is that you may find it stimulating and worthwhile and, when you come to the end, that you will be glad you read it.


John Devlin,
November, 2000.

*Please don't tell, no, no, no*
*Don't say that I told you so*
*I just heard a rumour from a friend*

*I don't say that it's true*
*I'll just leave that up to you*
*If you don't believe, I'll understand*

*from "Peggy Sue Got Married"*

*Buddy Holly, 1958.*

# The
# Devil's
# Vortex

# Prologue

It was quiet in the wee small hours, as quiet as Manhattan ever gets. The towering sentinel buildings sighed in their loneliness in the cold clear night air while the lights on the giant Christmas tree in Rockefeller Center sparkled out across the sunken skating rink. Bereft now of it's lively, colourful skaters, the rectangle of ice giving off a frozen deathly white glow as though it was entombed by the enclosing skyscrapers. In the surrounding streets, the occasional taxicab moved like a lazy prowling cat, freed of the daytime roar of traffic and the fight for space.

Outside the Sheraton Center Hotel, the tiny decorative white lights on the stark, bare branches of the trees shimmered in the sharply cold night air, like clouds of dancing constellations. Inside the cosy warmth of the hotel, the guest rooms were almost all in darkness. Room 3421 was quiet and dark, it's lone inhabitant asleep.

Tom Ryan hadn't yet woken, nor was he still asleep, but he was now sitting up in bed in the near total darkness of his room, the silence broken only by his own gasping, choking scream. He did not know where he was, or what he was. He could have been on Mars or been a fish, a stone or anything or nothing. Every sensory reference point had gone, all sense of conscious being had gone, there was no sense of time. He was drifting unconnected in some dark emptiness, aware only of a sickening fear. He'd stopped breathing.

Desperately what was left of him fought to control the cascading panic, pull himself back, identify with something, grasp and hold on to anything to find himself again. He became aware of the thin outline of light coming into the room around the edges of the curtains. His eyes locked on, staring fixedly, in case the light slipped away into something meaningless and left him lost and drifting again. Slowly, slowly as though caught in the turbulence of a powerful stream, he was vomited back into the oozing organic universe of smells and flesh as his tumbling thoughts gathered together and clung to themselves in little groupings and they in turn joined to form larger related groups, eventually forming a structure and then the world rushed back to him like some giant overpowering tidal wave. This was New York, the Sheraton Center Hotel, Christmas Week, 1994. The sound of his rasping scream still reverberated in the room as he started to breath again, his whole body shaking, weak and soaked in sweat. But just as the familiarity of the real world established itself again, he was overtaken by a new feeling of terror, realizing he had just escaped one nightmare only to re-enter the reality of another. The IRA were going to kill him.

He switched on the bedside light and sank back exhausted into the bed, listening to the coarse sound of his breathing and staring up at the ceiling trying to calm himself then confirm the objects in the room in the soft reflections of the comforting lightly patterned beige and gold wallpaper. Another thought surfaced in the turmoil of his mind about his brother telling him once when they were young, everything is just energy. He pushed it away, he didn't want that now, go away and let me see and find a solid reliable world. He sought out each object, the wall lights, the pictures on the walls, the chairs, saw the dark brown of the table with the reflected light like a silver streak along it's edge, wanting everything around him to be solid and three dimensional. He turned and grabbed at his travel clock from beside the bed, watching the second hand step, step, step, across the clear dial with its organization of numbers measuring the regularity of time. It was 3.15am. He wished to God that Kara was here to hold him, put her arms around him, to feel the warmth of another human being, to feel the soft animal comfort of another living thing, to find sanctuary. But he knew there was no sanctuary to be found for him, not now.

He started to half remember his decisions of yesterday, to check out of the hotel as soon as possible and without drawing attention to himself. Maybe 6.00am he'd thought, and then move on. In the panic of his escape from Ireland, pressurized by events, this hotel had seemed an obvious choice, the one he knew well, the one he always used when he was in Manhattan. Despite the external stark modern appearance, the Sheraton Center was like and old slipper to him, familiar, somehow like coming home after the disconnection of the long transatlantic flight. But he would be too easily found here, too many people he worked with used it as a convenient base for business. But he'd had to give US Immigration some idea of what he was doing here and a contact address. For this, the Sheraton was as good as anything else. He must now try to distance himself, keep moving, leave as few traces as possible. He must try to make disconnected jumps, try to shake the trails off. Credit cards, they would be another problem, too easily traced, he needed to disappear from all records. He had tried to think about all this on the flight and it had all raced through his mind again before going to sleep. Yesterdays thoughts started to come back now, half remembered, problems left hanging. He needed to think, but a weary sense of isolation gripped him now, accentuating the fear with loneliness.

He got out of bed and went into the bathroom, ran the cold tap and splashed the freezing cold water onto his face and the back of his neck. As he straightened up and drew the soft white hotel towel down his face, he looked uneasily into the mirror that nearly covered the entire wall, and took stock of the image it portrayed. The man who looked back was about six foot tall and his brown hair was showing the signs of threatening grey, the thin face drawn and haggard, the disturbed troubled eyes showing the lack of sleep and betraying his mental state. For the first time he was outside the organization he had given his life to, was now despised as the lowest of the low, a traitor. There was no sanctuary now, and he thought how he would be hunted as common prey by both the security forces and the IRA. There were no safe connections, he was cut-off. It wasn't the inevitable subterfuge that troubled him, subterfuge was familiar, but this was different, he was outside everything and separated from everyone now, alone. In danger and bringing danger with him wherever he went and to every contact, seeing danger everywhere and in every contact. What, he wondered were his chances of survival? Slight at best, he thought, even those defecting from the IRA with the security forces to protect them, to provide them with funds and new identities at regular intervals and new locations, even they were not safe. All it took was one careless move, one careless remark by a friend, or one betrayal.

Tom Ryan wondered if maybe he had made a bad mistake, allowed himself to be pressurized into panic? Maybe he should have stayed, continued on as normal. He held the towel to his eyes and shook his head. No, he told himself, it had been the only decision, to cut and run, it had an inevitable logic to it, if you could talk of logic at all. He hadn't been able to find an alternative, there was no alternative, he knew that, the problem had pounded and twisted through his mind in the days before leaving Ireland. Only now he was confronted with the awful reality of the irrevocable step he had taken, been forced to take. He was on his own, isolated, at risk. At risk of a death that would not likely be clean, for death he knew was rarely clean or quick. He shivered at the prospect and the knowledge that it could come anytime, anywhere.

He turned on the cold tap again and soaked the towel then held it to his face, feeling the shock of the stinging cold. As he continued to hold the towel to his face and forced himself to bring the cold towel round again to the back of his neck, he thought of the robbery, picturing Maguire, seeing the carnage with it's wasted lives, and then the spilling uncontrollable chaos that had erupted in the wake of this mayhem to turn and threaten him. It was all crazy, there were no explanations for what had gone wrong, but the consequences were all his now. Running in confusion, hoping to gain time, trying to stay alive, wanting to live, taste life again, taste love again. He saw himself in the mirror, the scar on the left hand side of his face, running down parallel to his ear, looking dull red and obvious, as it always did in winter. It was the best the surgeons had been able to do all those long years ago and it had become so much apart of him that he normally didn't notice it at all. He pulled the cold wet towel away from around his neck and saw the remaining marks where the bullet had entered his left shoulder.

Then his mind was set racing with frantic thoughts of what needed to be done, decisions that had to be made if he was to have any chance of survival, of finding a way out. There would be no more sleep for him to-night. He decided he couldn't wait until morning, he must put the next move in place right away.

He went back into the bedroom and started pulling on his clothes, thinking back to the strange nightmarish experience that had visited him in his sleep. Whatever it was, it was not like the familiar nightmares that periodically sought him, those that haunted him from the reality of his life thirty years before. Those he knew well and knew their origins all too clearly, seventeen years of age and lying in a field in Northern Ireland on a wet cold winters night being kicked by the armed police until he was sick with the pains running through his whole body and slipped into unconsciousness, or being dragged out of a prison cell in Belfast to be beaten whenever a bomb went off in a mailbox in England. These events and the remembered shattering fear had been engraved into his young mind and now when they slipped out of his conscious mind for a while, they sometimes came back in sleep, distorted but still easily recognizable for their origins.

Sitting on the edge of the bed as he tied his shoelaces, he
tried to shake off the residual feelings of horror. Finally
dressed, he put on his coat and left the room. Walking
through the warm deserted corridors, his footsteps silent in
the deep pile carpet, the peacefulness of the hotel was
broken only by the ice-making machine with its rumbling
sounds of permanent indigestion. Peace. How long was it
now, four months, the IRA cease-fire had been in place
now for almost four months. There had been times, in fact
for most of his life, he had never thought to see it happen.
It was truly extraordinary, a miracle, the transformation to
peace in Northern Ireland, but it would be of no help to
him. In fact, as he knew only too well, the cease-fire was
going to make his position all the more dangerous. His was
an internal IRA matter and maintenance of discipline during the cease-fire was a priority and he knew that the military resources to track him down would be all the more
easily available. Somehow he had to manage to stay alive
and gain time in the vague hope of somehow finding a solution. The fear of the uncontrollable nature of the problem
that confronted him, seeped like fingers of cold into his
bones as he walked down the long straight hotel corridor
from his room. Ahead of him there was the sharp sound of
a door opening and the corridor was immediately a killing
ground. He threw himself flat against the wall. The pretty
young woman leaving the room looked back and smiled at
him as she closed the door after her and continued on her

way about her business. He didn't move, just leaned back limp, his heart pounding, trying to put himself back together again and then made his way to the elevator.

Outside the hotel, the intense cold of the night air bit into Tom Ryan's face and seeped through his coat, reminding him that his coat was inadequate for the extremes of a New York winter. He reckoned it should be approaching ten o'clock at night in Hawaii, there was a good chance of making contact. He reached an intersection with a payphone and asked the operator to make a collect call. While he stood shivering and waiting to be connected, a cop car cruised down the street and stopped at the intersection light, a vapour cloud pluming from the exhaust and hanging in the air. They took a good look at him and he remembered he had left the room without his wallet or any form of identification. If they decided to question him now about what he was doing on the street at 4am it could be disastrous, he couldn't afford to end up on a police report. He turned away as though talking into the phone. He heard the low throaty rumble of the engine as the police car slowly pulled away. Even the New York cops would know about the robbery and the carnage in Ireland, all the more so as an Irish cop was now among the dead. He could only hope his luck would hold and they would drive on and not check him out. The phone line came alive again as the phone started ringing in Hawaii and Tom Ryan tried to push the thoughts of the robbery out of his mind.

# Chapter 1

The meat plant robbery had been set-up for Thursday, two weeks before Christmas, 1994. On the night of the robbery, Tom Ryan was in his apartment on the fourth floor of the newly built block, overlooking the small town of Castleglen and with a view of the surrounding mountains in the background. He had phoned Kara, telling her he was going to bed early as he had a busy day to-morrow, Friday, but that he was looking forward to seeing her and how they would spend the weekend together in Dublin. At 11.30pm he was watching television, yet another political discussion about Northern Ireland and the continuing IRA cease-fire. It would be another two hours before he needed to leave for the drop site, but he knew that the pieces of the action were already falling into place.

*     *     *

The dark blue, four door family car was parked on a small, twisting hillside road with a good view of the entire meat processing plant. The concrete apron surrounding the plant buildings was brightly illuminated as the heavy trucks were loaded and then pulled out to start their journey from the rural town of Castleglen in the mid-west of Ireland. All heading to the continental ferries and the cities of Europe in time for the busy Christmas trade. The young English-man, Jones, sat in the front passenger seat beside Joe who would drive to-night. Jones was smoking, the window beside him half open. Even his thick reddish blonde hair, cut short, standing straight up from his head but retaining a slight wave, irritated the older man, Maguire, who sat in the back of the car. Danny Maguire told himself that he had been out with worse and that he would cope. He looked away, out through the car window. It looked like it might rain before the night was out.

"How much longer?" Jones asked in his Birmingham accent, turning his head to the right, towards the driver, but the question was addressed to Maguire,

"Maybe an hour maybe a little less" Maguire replied.

"How can you be sure the other security guard is taken out? We should have had a phone with us, we don't even know if Ryan is in place"

"The younger security guard will be accounted for in the pub as arranged, my man is entirely reliable. And Ryan will be in place for the pick-up because Tom Ryan is entirely reliable. And we don't have a phone because I've no plans to phone any sex lines to-night and neither do I intend to inform the listening public or your former friends in the British Army what we're doing or let them know where we

are. And we're here early because I'm always early to make
bloody sure we have no surprises. I've been at this since
before you were born and with your kind assistance we will
no doubt get through this little exercise to-night."

"Who is this guy taking out the guard then, it seems we are
totally relying on him for that part of the operation?"

"That's my business, not yours or anyone else's. Even Joe
doesn't get involved there. It's a personal arrangement,
directly with me and no one else."

There was silence for a while, until Jones spoke again,
"This bloke you have, he isn't one of us, what's his connection then?"

"Like I said, it's personal, we go back a long way. When
we were both very young, we learned our business the hard
way as a couple of Minders in the East End of London. In
that business, you learnt to trust each other."

"Like in the Army then?"

"Aye, something like that. But, of course, I don't have your
intimate knowledge of serving with Her Majesty's forces",
replied Maguire.

*     *     *

Seymour had entered the pub at 9.30. It was getting busy as he expected. The busier it was the better he liked it. It had taken him an hour and a half from Dublin to the village of Castleglen. After parking the motorcycle in a corner at the dark outer edge of the car park, he took off his riding gear and left it in the panniers. Now he looked like everyone else. He took a quick look around the car park before he came into the pub. He knew the local crowd would immediately identify him as a stranger with their well practiced and seemingly casual sidelong glances of curiosity. He went to the bar and ordered a pint of Guinness. Two customers got up and vacated a table in an alcove and Seymour sat himself down. From there he had a view of the entire bar opposite which ran almost the length of the pub. Like so many, the pub had started life as a nice simple traditional country pub, been modernized to vinyl and plastics in the late Fifties and had now been put back to something of an imitation of it's former self with off-the-shelf pub interiors. The result was artificial and ugly, but functional and no doubt more efficient.

He looked at his watch, it would be another half hour before Sheila and Madden came to join him. The money for the job was good enough and, all in all, it wasn't much different from what he did for much the rest of his working life for various clients. But he'd prefer not to be involved in this, even on the periphery. If it wasn't for Maguire. Well if it wasn't for Danny Maguire he wouldn't be alive and that was the start and the end of it. Maguire had already been working for the gangland boss in London when Seymour got the job as his assistant. Gangland London was rough in the Sixties, even for Seymour who was very fit and already well skilled in taking care of himself. One night he'd got on the wrong side of a club owner and if Maguire hadn't intervened and taken out two men, Seymour would have met death early and very painfully. He thought that after all these years, he must ask Maguire sometime how he had found him that night. No one had been more surprised than Seymour to see him walk in. Big, easy and strong, totally confident. After that, they both got out of London. But the association continued, such bonds were not easily broken. So here he was to-night. Just another job.

He saw Sheila and Madden come in,
"How are we doing?" Madden inquired, smiling broadly and looking like he was casually meeting up for an evenings drinking.

"You're a little early, our friend hasn't arrived yet, get yourselves a drink."

A little later, Seymour saw McArthur come in, young and cocky and sure he could handle himself. Along with the picture, Maguire had given Seymour a little background information. McArthur was a former Irish Army boxing champion, before becoming a security guard at Castleglen Meats. They waited until he was almost finished his second pint, getting nice and talkative and assertive with the locals at the bar. Oh well, Seymour thought, better get it over with and then nodded to the others,

"OK, let's get on with the performance, remember I'll take care of it myself, you two just make the occasion for me and cover my back."

It was a performance they had given before, Sheila and Madden went to the bar for more drinks and on the way back Sheila did her provocative sexy act as she wriggled through the crowd past McArthur who made a mild enough remark. But it was all they needed, the opening had been made, the scene rolled on. The barman said he didn't want any trouble in here, so the fight took place in the carpark. The security guard was a little embarrassed, this skinny old guy looked entirely harmless. The types who usually took him on, all reckoned they rated themselves and looked the part. But this guy, it was ridiculous, damn near insulting for him. He really wasn't very interested, but he was sure it would be over very quickly and it was. The thing was, he couldn't understand how he ended up on the ground with a broken arm and a dis-jointed knee in less than five seconds after it started. His supporting onlookers were equally surprised and there was complete silence except for the guard moaning slightly and trying to hold his knee. Seymour thought it best to add a few words of abuse before slipping away from the crowd, just to hold up the illusion a little while longer. Sheila and Madden were already moving out towards the car they had parked at the side of the road a short distance from the pub carpark. They kept observation, giving Seymour time to change back into his bike gear and made sure no one interfered with him as he rode out on the big new, red sports BMW R1100RS, turning fast out of the carpark, accelerating hard onto the road back for Dublin. He kicked the gear shift up into fifth at eighty, twisted the throttle and felt the full engine torque bite through the back wheel, the adrenaline rush from the fight still pumping through him, the bike rocketed forward, hungry for the road. The wind howled around his helmet and he pushed himself back along the seat, tucking his body down behind the sport fairing. No one would catch him. The job was done. He was away.

\*     \*     \*

On the far side of the town of Castleglen, Joe, the driver, took a cloth out of the glove compartment and wiped the condensation from the inside of the car window so they could see clearly as the last of the trucks pulled out. Without the trucks, the Castleglen Meats plant looked eerie, the external loading lights giving a yellowish hue to the concrete apron and the buildings behind. The cars of the late shift workers now quickly followed, streaming out of the entrance gates past the brightly lit central island formed by the gatehouse, all anxious to make it to the pubs in time for a drink or two. The three men in the car watched the scene from their vantage point and saw the lone, middle aged security guard start to make his way around the now deserted plant, systematically switching off the lights in each section as he checked it.

Jones inquired,

"How long more is it going to take that old bastard to lock up?"

Maguire replied in his quiet, deep and easy voice, sounding almost sleepy, disinterested and detached from the world,

"That old bastard is Ed Williams. I went to school here with him. He's not the brightest, but he likes his job and is careful and he'll be finished shortly. Just take it easy now Jones."

\*    \*    \*

Ed Williams made his way back to the gatehouse and put on the kettle for tea. It was 12.30. He wondered what had happened to his younger assistant, McArthur, what excuse would there be this time for missing the shift. He switched on the small black portable radio that had become his companion in these long nights. He didn't need McArthur anyway, he enjoyed the feeling of being in charge of this bright new plant, the freedom from idle chatter, the peace and quiet to make up the records of truck movements in and out of the plant. The music from the local radio station was drowned out by the screech of his kettle as it came to the boil. Sitting down again with his cup of tea, his mind wandered to the prospect of Christmas and family and he picked up the evening newspaper which he had left folded on the table when he started his shift.

He didn't see or hear them arrive, but he looked up to see the gun pointing straight at him through the open car window behind the driver. The masked figure slowly shook its head and said softly,
"Now Mr. Williams, take it nice and easy and don't move an inch or I'll have to blow you away."

The guard believed him. The threatening black image with slits for eyes and mouth, and pointing the gun at him, looked like the TV pictures he'd seen of the IRA and UVF wall paintings in Belfast. Dear God no, he thought, not them. The guy beside the driver got out and came forward pointing another gun at him. Ed Williams had never seen a gun before. Jones wrenched the phone off the cradle and said,
"Now open the fuckin' gate, get the keys of the plant and you just might live to see the New Year."
Williams had difficulty understanding the Birmingham accent, he looked back blankly and didn't move. With his

left hand, Jones grabbed him by his jacket, pulling him close and pressed the gun to the side of his head. Ed Williams held up the keys for Jones to see, the whole bunch gangling and making a tinkling sound. Jones pushed him out of the gatehouse and towards the car.

Jones bundled Williams in through the back door beside Maguire. They drove up to the office block and went in. Williams was sweating now as he turned off the alarm system with Jones pressing the cold hard barrel of the gun to the side of his head. Maguire, Jones and the guard walked through the corridors of the deserted office block and went into the room with the safe. Maguire gestured to Jones, "Take him back and tie him to the chair in reception and let's get going on this."

Jones took the guard back to the entrance and tied his hands behind him and to the chair with a length of detonator wire. Meanwhile Maguire got out the explosives and placed the charges against the hinges of the safe. Jones came back in to see Maguire playing out the run of detonator wire. Maguire handed him the reel of wire and said, "Take it two offices down, this little bang will take out the windows and possibly half the walls as well."

The safe blew with an almighty roar and they went back into the room. The safe door was on the floor, bent and with pieces missing off the sides with the force of the explosion. There was plaster hanging off the walls, the false ceiling panels hung loose and the room was full of the choking fumes of the explosive mixed with plaster dust. They made their way towards the safe with flashlights, climbing across the scattered debris of what was left of the office interior. The cash had been delivered that afternoon and was still in its bank wrappers, neat bundles ready to pack into their holdall. Maguire looked at the piles of banknotes and whistled softly,

"My God, the Christmas bonuses and the overtime pay must be well up on what was expected, this is looking good! Bring over that desk so we can put the bag on it and help me load."

They were almost finished when they heard the alarm go off, sounding like it would wake the entire countryside. Maguire glared at Jones,

"What the fuck — how could that happen — the guard, did you tie him securely?"

They ran out to the reception area only to be confronted by an empty chair. Maguire, furious now, sensing that his careful planning was about to be derailed,

"Jesus! Get after the fucker."

Jones hesitated,

"He can't have gone out the front, Joe's out there, he must have gone into the plant. Let's leave him and get out."

But Maguire wasn't in the mood for new plans,
"I told you to get after him, Christ only knows what he's up to he's still got the fucking keys with him. I'm not having this fucked up."

They ran through the offices, back through the building towards the factory, switching on the lights as they entered each section. Arriving from different directions they found Ed Williams huddled on the floor beside the large white door of a floor-to-ceiling refrigerator. His hands were still loosely joined by the wire. Jones was behind him, Maguire in front. Williams stared down at the floor, his entire body shaking. Before Maguire could say anything, Jones put a bullet through the top of the guard's bald head. Every limb in the body went into convulsions and the wire tore through the frantically pulling hands. Blood and brain material came out through the top of the head, oozing out over the tight white shiny skin. The hands enmeshed in the wire were becoming a convulsive bloody mess. Maguire, shouting now,
"Jesus, you bastard, that was fucking stupid and unnecessary."

"I thought you wanted this tidied up."

"What the fuck are you trying to prove Jones?"

Maguire stepped forward and put another shot through the

side of the head. As he stepped back from the now still body and while the sharp sound of the gunshot reverberated around the Cold Storage Area, Maguire's two way communications set bleeped and they heard Joe's voice,

"We have company. A black Mercedes has just arrived at the entrance and I can see the lights of a squad car coming down the road. Come out the back, I'm bringing the car 'round."

Jones asked Maguire, "What about the money?"

"It's too fucking late for that, we can't go back now unless you're thinking of taking out a few coppers as well."

Maguire and Jones made their way to the back of the plant and got into the car. Joe drove around to the side of the plant so that they could see what was happening at the entrance. They waited in the car with the lights out until they saw the police car drive in. Seeing the lights on in the plant and the Mercedes parked outside, the two local cops ran straight into the building. Joe eased the car quietly out through the front gates and then accelerated briskly once they were clear of the plant entrance. No one came after them. They were clear.

As they drove, Maguire turned to Joe and asked, "Any idea who was in the Mercedes?"

"It can only have been the new plant manager, Prender-gast, he lives quite close by. He must have had an alarm monitor installed, otherwise he couldn't have got here so quick."

"OK Joe, slow down and take it steady, let's try to avoid attention for the moment. We'll make for the escape car and clear the area. The only thing that matters now, is to remain cool and get clear of this fucking shambles."

They drove on steadily for another ten minutes. The time dragged, they were all edgy as they thought about the events of the night and how wrong it had all gone. Maguire knew the Army Council of the IRA would not be at all impressed and would hold him responsible. He also knew the politicos in the movement in general and O'Sullivan in particular, would be hysterical because of shooting Willi-ams. It wasn't good for public relations to have innocent middle-aged family men taken out in the course of fund raising. Maguire thought that if they could get clear away, the whole thing might be put down to the operation of a criminal gang. That, he decided was his only hope now, to minimize the damage caused by the failed operation.

Coming out of a small one street village, ahead of them they saw a police checkpoint. Just two unarmed cops, a portable "STOP" sign in the middle of the road and the police car parked at the side. The word had got out quickly, but it looked like the first alert was to a simple robbery, they mustn't have scaled up yet on the basis of finding the dead guard. Just a matter of time but so far so good. Maguire turned to Joe,

"Slow now Joe, like you're going to stop, then drive through fast."

As one of the cops came over to the almost stopped car, Joe put his foot to the floor and took off in second gear with the tyres screaming as he slipped the clutch under full power. Jones reached into his bag and lobed a hand grenade out of the side window. As the car rocketed forward it was followed down the road by the explosion. The rear window of the car imploded. Maguire turned round from the front seat and shot Jones between the eyes. There was a gasp of rapidly expelled air from Jones as his head was thrown back against the seat.

"That's the last mistake that fucking madman makes. We're in for it now. All hell will break loose around us, so much for minimizing the damage."

"Jesus!" was all Joe replied.

"Joe, the priority now is for the two of us to get clear, we should still be in with a chance now that we're not at risk from fucking 'Action Man' here."

"What about Tom Ryan? He'll be out at the drop site soon and know nothing about this."

"He'll be OK, he's an old hand and can look after himself. We can hardly stop off at the drop site and leave a note for him. When he finds nothing there, he'll figure out something has gone wrong. So long as he doesn't hang around too long he'll be OK."

Joe looked pale and shaken now, but he drove on fast and expertly until he turned off the main road and they started to climb up the steep track and into the State Forest. They reached the cleared forestry work area where the sleek, almost new, black Ford Cosworth was just as they had left it that afternoon when all their plans had still been fresh. The Ford looked much like any other car, belying the powerfully tuned engine and modified suspension underneath. It was Joe's pride and joy, a driver's car, a wolf in sheep's clothing. Joe and Maguire, poured petrol inside the first car, then changed into new clothes and torched the car with their old clothes and the body of Jones still on the back seat. As Joe drove the high performance Ford carefully down the uneven forest track and out onto the road again, he asked,

"Do you hear it?"

"What?"

"The chopper!"

"Sweet Jesus, now they know precisely where we are with that fucking car on fire."

Joe drove on, flat out now, and without looking at him, asked Maguire what they should do,

"Even in this I can't get away from a chopper, what do you reckon?"

"We'd best make for the coast, we might get away in McIntyre's trawler. Let's just hope he's in port and that he's sober."

Joe settled himself for the long haul to Galway and the single-minded task of driving the high performance car as fast as he knew how. With the roar of the car engine and the twisting narrow country roads, they couldn't be sure if the helicopter was tracking them.

"Joe, we need a fork in the road followed by some overhead cover like trees around an entrance gate, somewhere we can get in out of sight."

"Yeah, I think I know just the place, coming up soon."

They came to the fork in the road and went left, the tyres screaming as they took the bend for the minor road without slowing and found the entrance gates to the grounds of a large Georgian country house. The entrance gates were set back from the road in a high semi-circular granite wall surrounded by big mature trees. The car spun sending up showers of old gravel from the surface and finished up tight alongside one of the walls. Joe switched the lights and engine off. They could hear the helicopter coming closer, then circling. After a couple of minutes it went away and they drove back onto the main road again.

"I wish to Christ it would rain, Joe, rain good and hard."

"Yeah, it just might make the difference."

Twenty miles from the coastal port, a bleak overcast dawn started to light the sky. They were getting tired, but almost there. They took a fast bend in the road only to find they were heading straight into another check point, but this time the road was blocked with army trucks and police cars, there was no way out and they were travelling too fast. Joe got one set of wheels up on the pavement, changed down a couple of gears and fought to control the car as it bounced over the uneven surface. He saw the raised guns taking aim and shouted to Maguire,
"Get your head down!"

The shots cascaded around the car, one splintering Joe's thigh. He lost control and the car rolled over first bouncing down on the passenger side then over onto the roof. Sparks flew in the track of the screeching metal roof as it skidded along the road. Both of them had been hit now and in the struggle to maintain consciousness and control the pain, they could smell the petrol escaping from the overturned car. Maguire could hear Joe screaming now as he was hit again. His screams and the screeching of the roof blended into a single discordant and appalling background noise.

But for Danny Maguire it all started to recede, seem distant, everything had slowed down for him, he felt removed from reality, it was like looking at a movie. He could see the big wheels at the side of the army truck ahead. They were going to hit it. He felt strangely calm, he knew death was coming to meet him. Soon, it would be soon. He had faced death before, taken his chance with it, shot before he was shot, watched others die, sometimes quick and clean, sometimes slow, ugly and painful. Now he was sure this time it was for him. It was going to come. There was a burst of light inside the car as the petrol caught fire on the road. It seemed like just another part of the unfolding sequence of sound, image and dull pain. All remote, disconnected from him. He felt calm, almost bemused at what was about to happen. Almost certainly there would be no lingering. It would be quick when it came. An end to it all.

# Chapter 2

The town of Castleglen seemed pressed down, squashed by the rain that Friday morning as it's inhabitants ran for the shelter of their cars or waited, cold, irritable and sodden for the bus to take them to work. The rain came in a grey darkness, striking down through the air from unseen clouds in an unseen sky, and poured down walls and flooded in waves and rivulets across streets and pavements. But for once the wet huddled and running people of the town were not talking about the weather, the early morning radio news bulletins had started to relate the events of the previous night. There were no wry remarks about it being a soft morning, the deeds of the previous night were too horrific in this small community where everyone knew everyone else.

Just like everyone else in the town, Tom Ryan had listened to the news reports, but with an even keener interest than his neighbours. He was still trying to make a complete picture from the unfolding story being pieced together by the news reporters as he drove into the carpark of the Western Regional Development Agency. He'd had two hours uneasy sleep. He switched off the engine and the radio went dead disconnecting him from one world and sending him into another as he ran from his allotted car space

through the rain and puddles alongside the uninspiring single story industrial style building. Reaching the shelter of
the red brick and glass panelled reception area he was
greeted by a cheerful "Good Morning Mr. Ryan" from
Joan, the receptionist. Christ, he thought, shaking the rain
off himself, this is just another working day. He looked
across at her and smiled,

"Isn't it as well we have someone as beautiful as you Joan,
sitting there on this dreadful morning or no one would
come to see us at all!"

She smiled back at him, blushed and looked away, pre-
tending to be tidying her desk, glad of the attention from
this man she fancied. He was different from most of them
that worked there, she thought, still, you couldn't really say
you fancied someone his age. Perhaps she would just like
to have had him as a father, but then she thought, anyone
would have been better than the one she had whose idea
of life stopped at his farm gate and the price of bacon.

As he started down the corridor, he looked back at her. It
seemed to him that she inhabited a different world, one for
which he didn't have the entry requirements of being young
and female. He sighed to himself, his world seemed a lot
older and sadder than hers. Then he thought there was
never a time when his world was like hers, not even when
he was young.

The phones were always busy on a Friday morning. In these quiet few moments before 9am, the pretty young receptionist was free to think her happy thoughts of the weekend ahead, almost the last before Christmas and the holidays. She thought about the disco that she and her friends had agreed to go to that night, after the pub, who would be there. Her dreamy thoughts were more exciting than the routine of answering the phones. She had started thinking about Christmas when the phone rang again, and she answered injecting brightness into her standard, well-worn phrase,

"Good Morning, Western Regional Development Authority."

"And Good Morning to you too sweetheart. Would you kindly put me through to Tom Ryan and you can tell him it's a personal call."

Obnoxious slimy creep with a sharp Northern accent she thought as she connected him to Tom Ryan's office.

"Ryan."

"Did you get the money?"

O'Sullivan's voice, he could picture the fat little bastard, the young smooth face, round, like the features pushed into a piece of bread dough, the eyes magnified and hard behind the John Lennon glasses,

"For Christ's sake are you mad using this phone after what happened last night."

"The situation is hardly what you'd call normal, I fucking know we have three dead men Tom, did you get the money?"

It was the first Ryan knew that all three were dead, the earlier news reports had left him believing that one of the IRA group had survived and escaped,
"No, there was nothing there."

"What do you mean there was nothing there, they got the Ford, they had to go by the drop point?"

"I was there at 2.15am as planned. There was nothing there, I was lucky to get out of the area before the whole place was overrun by police and army."

"They're describing it as a fucking robbery, with a quarter of a million missing. Right, so the amount has probably been inflated as usual, but the fucking money is gone for sure. The lads must have got it and they must have left it, how is it possible you didn't pick it up? You haven't gone fucking chicken on us I hope? Your bloody soft views are only too well known in the organization."

Ryan breathed in and counted to five and controlled himself before answering,

"I went out as arranged. I'm telling you there was nothing there."

"Maybe you're just too fucking old for this now Tom. Even picking up a bag. Not like the old days when you had your little run up North, 'eh. At least, that's what I hope I'm hearing, for your sake. We play rough these days Tom. Three men died for that haul and we want the fucking proceeds. Every last penny of it. It's my responsibility to report back and I need answers and I need the cash accounted for. You'd better go out and look again. I'll be in touch. Remember, you're the one responsible for delivering the cash."

There was a brief tense silence before O'Sullivan put the phone down. In the silence, Tom Ryan began to understand the danger to himself. There was no attempt at subtlety, not that he would have expected subtlety from O'Sullivan, the threat was clear. Ryan was left still holding the beige telephone receiver, his elbows resting on his standard issue steel office desk, his eyes now fixed at some mid-point in the office space, the wall charts a blur, the face of O'Sullivan in his minds eye. There had always been a tension between O'Sullivan and the rest of the southern group, ever since he arrived from the North. Too young to have been actively involved in the cataclysmic events of '69, far too young for the IRA Campaign in the Fifties. In fact, O'Sullivan had never seen action, never put himself in danger. He was the original ambitious political apparatchik.

Slowly Ryan put the receiver down and sat back in his chair. Jesus, he thought, what the hell was going on? From the morning news reports he knew the security guard at the meat plant was dead, that there were two dead in the Ford and two cops in intensive care. Now O'Sullivan had told him all three of the IRA group were dead. It made no sense, this was to be a simple easy robbery. Instead everyone directly involved was dead and no sign of the cash. And now O'Sullivan was holding him responsible, had him cornered. Ryan wondered if they could have taken the cash with them in the Ford, there seemed no reason why they should, but neither was there an explanation for how the whole thing had gone so completely wrong. In the madness of last night, anything was possible. He knew it would be at least a couple of days before the IRA source in the Police Forensics Department found out what was in the first reports on the remains of the Ford. Perhaps the money was incinerated in the car, but it was a long shot. If Maguire had the cash, then he would surely have left it at the drop point, Maguire had always planned carefully. Ryan decided he could only wait and see what turned up in the remains of the car. But wait for how long, O'Sullivan was dangerous and in the end Ryan couldn't convince himself the cash was in the car. It all made no sense to him, he was left with the threatening voice of O'Sullivan ringing in his head.

The routine of the day was a welcome distraction, looking

for new opportunities to bring overseas industry into the area, assessing projects for their commercial potential, workforce requirements, training and these days the inevitable environmental impact assessment. His own special area was arranging financial facilities for the new projects. By five o'clock it all stopped for the ritual of the Friday after-work drink in the local pub. Outside, the rain too had stopped and the colourful lights of the modest Christmas tree in Reception glowed in happy gaudy celebration. The pub was already packed and everyone was in fine form, standing room only, the air heavy with smoke and the sound of laughter peeling out sporadically over the background rumble of busy conversations. Each one around the crowded bar pushing up against those seated on the barstools along the bar and trying to catch the eye of the overworked barmen to obtain another round of drinks. Then the balancing act as they ferried the drinks back to a table through the good-natured crowd.

Ryan was careful about how much he had to drink, the lack of sleep the previous night was starting to make itself felt. After some general discussion of the image problems caused for the area by last night's events and expressions of sympathy for the awful killing of the local man, Ed Williams, the conversation of the group moved on in the usual way, to office politics, the new projects they were each working to attract into the region. Then the talk became

more social and about how plans for Christmas were coming along, presents for the kids. Everyone was getting
slightly and happily drunk.

"Tom, did you hear the latest about that religious maniac
O'Mahony? He was holding one of his Born Again Charis-
matic Meetings in his office at lunchtime on Wednesday
when Farrell walked by with the group from the Korean
electronics company. Jaysus, you have to hand it to Farrell,
when the Koreans were staring into the office with their
mouths open looking at them all singing their heads off, he
told them it was a group bonding exercise."

Then another laughing voice,
"But did you here about Farrell and Noreen Doyle from
Accounts, you know, the skinny one with the pony tail?
Well he got back with her to her place one evening after
pouring a few drinks into her. He was getting into her bed
with her half undressed when he notices something called
"Women and Celibacy" on the bookshelf beside the bed.
That was it, blew his mind entirely, decided this was definitely not the scene for him. So he told her he had an awful
headache and went home. She's looking at him yet! Farrell
claims she's taken up celibacy in earnest now!"

More laughter. After it started to subside, Tom Ryan said,
"Noreen is OK, she was my secretary until she took the job
in the accounts department."

The laughter stopped and there was an uncomfortable silence before he stood up and continued,

"Anyway, I must ask you all to excuse me, I have to get to Dublin. See you on Monday, have a good weekend!"

As he turned and started to make his way towards the door, one of the group said,

"Well if you're off to Dublin, you'll be going East again I suppose"

Ryan just grinned back at the assembled grinning faces, they all realized that the absurd geographical correctness of the remark was a way of gently getting at him and letting him know that they all knew about his affair in Dublin. He must have been seen by one of them in Dublin with his Japanese lover, Kara. The whole damn country worked like a small village, it was a wonder that anything could be kept secret at all.

It had been just a normal Friday evening out with colleagues, just like all the ones before. During the day he had decided what to do. He was going to Dublin to see Maitland.

The cold of the night air hit him as he exited from the overheated pub and made for his car and the start of the two hour drive. As he cleared the town, his mind turned to the prospect of the meeting ahead and why he had decided it was necessary. The difficult thoughts ensured that he stayed awake as he drove through the dark night and the

narrow twisting roads, the past and the present linked rib-
bon-like. The turns and sweeping headlights provided the
emphatic pulse against which his thoughts pounded on,
keeping him totally occupied for the entire journey. A
meeting with Maitland was the only response he could
think of after the conversation with O'Sullivan. The contrast between O'Sullivan and the man he was going to see
could hardly have been greater.

*      *      *

Jonathan Turnbull Radcliffe Maitland was in a job that was
seemingly ordained for him, Professor of English at Trinity
College, Dublin. He was also very English and very much
upper class. After his postdoctoral fellowship in Anglo-
Irish Literature at Harvard, he had offers of professorships
at Harvard, Oxford and Trinity College Dublin. His well to
do family were perhaps slightly bemused by his choice of
Dublin, but then the Maitlands were all used to independence of choice in their lives and they all knew that he
was perfectly capable of looking after himself without any
interference from them. The Trinity Board had done all
they could with the comparatively limited resources available to them to ensure his Chair was well funded and they
were delighted and somewhat surprised to find he accepted
their offer. The delight was particularly evident with those
more senior Board members who had for many years been
concerned about the numbers of staff they were recruiting

from the newer red-brick universities in Britain, or "The Mainland" as so many of them referred to it. Jonathan Maitland would do something to redress the balance and at least the standard of spoken English would improve at staff meetings, some of the new recruits they regarded as almost illiterate. So they looked forward to an improved "ethos" and improved academic standards. Altogether it seemed most satisfactory. Maitland was just twenty-eight years old when he accepted their offer.

Jonathan Maitland had sufficient inherited family money to ensure he could maintain a lifestyle only envied by his fellow academics from more humble financial backgrounds. Those of a more radical persuasion, viewed him with a mixture of disgust and envy. But such views were not evident in his presence, his quick cutting wit and crisp English tones were not to be experienced twice by those who had not already developed a healthy respect for his reputation. Not that any of this was, in itself, much different from the general bitchiness and envy of academic life. To his colleagues, the oddest thing about him was that he had learned and become perfectly fluent in "Gaelic" as he called it. He could change from his usual crisp clear tones in spoken English to the softer flowing resonance of his spoken Gaelic. He could even change from one Gaelic dialect to another while conducting conversations with people from different regions of Ireland. The English upper class was, of course, well known for it's fascination with odd languages and eccentricities of all sorts and that's how this oddity in his character was viewed by many of his colleagues. Just a mild and charming eccentricity that nicely complimented his brilliance in his chosen field of Anglo-Irish Literature. For his part, Maitland explained that he wanted to feel comfortable in his new home.

Under his guidance, his department grew in size and stature and was appropriately well funded by the College and handsomely supplemented by big business wishing to bask in the favourable light of being associated with such a distinguished and eminent scholar. Not for him the television and radio chat-show appearances of populist academics, his connections to the old establishment in Oxford and Cambridge and to the newer elite in Harvard, provided all of the right contacts he needed. He occasionally had to serve on Government appointed and University appointed committees, but, while he enjoyed the cut and thrust of University life, this type of committee tedium he kept to a minimum and it was obvious to all that Maitland fitted perfectly into the academic life of the University. In pushing his staff into the limelight of publicity he was regarded as displaying the generosity that only a minority of the more able and self-confident academics are capable of. As a consequence he was rarely seen in press photographs or the annual graduation photographs and never seen on television. All of which suited him well as in addition to his busy academic life, he also served at the very highest level of the IRA. But that was known only to three people. Two of them were on the Army Council. The other was Tom Ryan.

The College Porter had been told by Professor Maitland that he was expecting a late visitor and the Porter vaguely recognized Tom Ryan as he raised the entrance gate for him and waved him through, but there were so many people over the years, it was impossible to place them all. It was 8.30pm when Tom parked the car in one of the spaces marked "visitor". Maitland had his suite of offices in the older part of the College, Front Square. This was jealously dominated by the Arts Faculties and the Administration. The Sciences and other more vocationally oriented faculties were kept to the outer periphery of the beautifully laid out grounds and squares of this old university. Maitland's suite of offices were of a size which reflected his high standing in the College, but he had privately furnished them to his own standards and tastes and there were always beautiful arrangements of fresh flowers throughout the offices. No one in College had rooms like these. No one else could afford to.

As soon as Ryan knocked on the door of the outer office, the door was almost immediately opened and the tall imposing figure of Maitland greeted him, a sheaf of papers in his hand,

"My dear Tom, how good to see you, it's really been far too long. Do come in. Will you join me in a glass of sherry — don't worry, not the poisonous College variety of flavoured acetic acid, you will be quite safe with this."

They went into the larger inner office, a vase of large bright yellow flowers brightening a corner against the contrasting dark wood panelling. Maitland poured the sherry and passed a glass to Ryan. The two men seated themselves on either side of Maitland's large antique desk. The Professor and his visitor,

"Thank you Jonathan, good of you to see me at such short notice."

"So how are things on the Industrial front, still bringing in lots of German and Japanese companies — the entire country will be changed before long if you keep this up. But I mustn't complain, they will all send their children here and we can talk to them about the joys of English Literature. You know the Sanyo Bank has been really most generous in funding the new Joyce Summer School. Quite what some of their executives make of "Finnigan's Wake" is all is rather beyond me, but then some of my opposite number in Oxford make an awful hash of even "Ulysses". By the way, did you hear about the Japanese chap who is translating "Finnigan's Wake" into Japanese? Really quite extraordinary, how will he go about it?"

Maitland sipped his sherry from the old and delicately cut leaded glass, his careless trivial chitter-chatter conversation contrasting with the sharp observant look in his eyes. He continued,

"Terrible to hear about that business last night in your area, frightful about the unfortunate guard. Poor man. I do hope it does not affect you too much."

Tom knew that was as close as Maitland would come to discussing anything of a sensitive nature within these four walls, the remark was just sufficient to indicate to Tom that Maitland had a very good idea what he was here about. It was clear that Maitland hadn't survived this long without exercising the most extreme care, somehow it all seemed to fit the pernickety academic personality as well. He continued his general easy going conversation with Tom,

"Perhaps when you have finished your sherry, we might walk across to see the extension to the New Library. I'm sure you will be interested to see the changes since you were last here. It's a most remarkable piece of work and we were terribly lucky to get funding."

They left the old granite buildings and started to walk slowly along the cobbled pathway enclosing the manicured lawns of Front Square. In the relative safety of darkness and the open outdoors, Maitland's tone changed to become more serious, more businesslike and quieter,

"So Tom, I presume your visit may be in some way connected with the little problem of last night?"

"Yes Jonathan, I'm sorry to bother you with it, but this looks serious even beyond the obvious disaster of the operation itself."

"I see, do go on."

"The operation went totally wrong. All three of our men are dead, the security guard is dead and the two police at the check-point are in a critical condition."

"Yes, that much is in the public domain at this stage."

"I've never known an operation like this to go so wrong. Danny Maguire knew well what he was doing and was a stickler for planning. But on top of all that, the funds from the robbery are missing and I am being held responsible."

"Ah."

"It's not clear what happened, but I was to pick up the funds at the drop point and there was certainly nothing there. It's one we've used before and we should have had no problem, even with the chaotic situation that seems to have developed last night. The most likely explanation, if you can call it that, is that they took the bag in the final car and it was destroyed in the inferno. But we won't know for sure till we get to see what's in the forensic report."

"Yes indeed. Any remains of the bag should show up easily enough in the forensic examination of the contents of the car."

"In the meanwhile O'Sullivan is putting pressure on me. He doesn't believe the boys didn't make the drop. At the moment I have to agree with him, there's no explanation for why the cash didn't arrive at the drop point. From all we know, they should have been able to leave the cash as arranged."

"Yes, I see. Mr. O'Sullivan can be difficult from what I hear. You know, of course, I have only a very indirect influence these days. The whole campaign has gone very hard, it's not like the early days. The robbery for example. I can understand the arguments of the military wing, but such things are ill advised in the cease-fire. There is a tendency to be far too quick, not look carefully and plan carefully. The cease-fire is still holding, though only just. But the growing impatience from our own military side is already only too obvious. They don't really believe the negotiations will go anywhere. And the Army Council currently contains a number of men of quite limited, how shall I put it, foresight, shall we say? The "Young Turks" believe they know it all. Just pour on more and more extreme measures and

they believe they can get results. Of course we all appreciate that there will be difficulties of all sorts in this process,
but it really is quite trying at times. The struggle has been
going on for so long now, the organization is having difficulty in controlling elements with psychopathic and criminal tendencies in addition to all the usual problems in this
type of process."

They turned the corner and started walking along by the
old red brick terrace of buildings, the "Rubrics", the com-
ings and goings of students releasing shafts of light from
the doorways and the sounds of youthful conversation and
laughter,

"But I have a very specific problem now, I need help in
keeping O'Sullivan off, I'm seriously worried about what
he might do."

"Yes. I'll do what I can, of course, but you must be careful,
the situation could easily get out of control. The cease-fire
is a kind of vacuum and the in-fighting in the Council for
power makes things very unstable. My advice is don't leave
yourself exposed for too long."

"But what can I do? If they believe I have the funds, the
consequences are inevitable. I may not be able to prove
that I never received them. O'Sullivan won't wait long."

"Yes, the situation is tricky. Now let's see, there are really two problems here. The first is to keep you alive for a little while longer, the second is to find or possibly replace the funds. The trouble is that this current kettle of fish will inevitably cause serious problems for the organization. It's not the sort of thing they want at all and it will only serve to open up old divisions about strategy. That means instability. All I can do is to give some general advice to our colleagues to remain calm and not take precipitive action to make matters worse. They will expect something of the sort from me with the furore that is already breaking out in the media. But with O'Sullivan in the picture, I can't be sure that anything I can do will guarantee your personal safety."

They turned and started through the narrow passage into Library Square.

"What can I do?"

"I really think you must get out, certainly within the next few days. That will, of course, have the immediate effect of making matters very much worse for you. You have to get the funds and return them to the organization. If you are successful in getting your hands on the necessary amount, I will use what influence I have to get you a hearing before the Army Council. How about your brother in the States, he might be able to help? You are close, aren't you, and he has done well for himself?"

The awful simplicity and starkness of Maitland's analysis stunned Ryan, perhaps all the more so because he had hoped it wouldn't come to this. Running was something that appalled him, it put him into a sub-human category as far as the tradition of the IRA was concerned,

"Jim doesn't like this sort of thing at all, doesn't share my politics and remembers all too clearly the problems the family had when I was caught in the border raid in the Fifties and jailed. He left a long time ago to get out of the place. His home is the States and apart from the Patrick's Day nonsense, he doesn't want to know."

"I'd help myself Tom, but I don't have that amount as immediately available liquid assets. As you know, two of my brothers are in positions in the British Establishment and this can be helpful to me in my special activities here. But my other brother looks after the family banking business, and he ensures that I don't leave substantial amounts lying around in current accounts. In any event, as you yourself are well aware, there are too many arms of government these days who take a keen interest in movements of substantial amounts between accounts and also any large cash transactions."

Tom started to realize how far Maitland was removed from the practicalities of it all, from the rough and tumble of what happened on the ground, perhaps everyone was powerless in the situation, he wondered what had he expected of Maitland anyway,

"Thank you Jonathan, and I do appreciate the thought, but I really came for your advice."

"Of course Tom and you are most welcome to anything I can do, but if the funds aren't immediately available, you must get out and give yourself some opportunity to find the amount. I'm saying this as someone who can perhaps take a more objective view than you can right now. It is not advice I give you lightly, once you've run, the die is cast, so to speak. You are then in a position where you have to come up with the funds and give a full explanation of what happened. But that is your only chance as I see it. The combination of the missing funds and the fact that the entire operation was taken out seems most suspicious. It can only be highly dangerous for you. The possibility that you have been set-up by someone seems real to me."

"Like O'Sullivan?"

"Possibly. He is part of a new element in the organization. By himself, I would have thought he didn't have the brains. I had believed they moved him down here because he was becoming a nuisance in the North, particularly with the delicate nature of the cease-fire. He was too keen on arranging embarrassing street demonstrations. But there are those who would like to remove anyone with a moderate tendency. Maybe someone has in mind to clear us all out. It's certainly one of the possibilities. Whatever the reason, you are now in an exposed and vulnerable position."

They went up the steps and entered the New Library.

# Chapter 3

It was that short lull in time, the brief period of near tranquillity, between the rush of traffic out of Dublin on a Friday evening and when the tide turned and the city centre street would become alive with it's assorted visiting night owls, each hunting in the darkness of the night. The parked car with the two bulky men in it had been there for four hours and was now looking all the more obvious as most of the parking spaces along the street cleared. Seymour looked down at them from his top floor office window. He was alone at the end of the day, and had turned his mind to his latest developing problem after dealing with the residue of the day's more or less routine items. Earlier in the afternoon, just as it was getting dusk and it had stopped raining, he had seen a traffic warden as she had tried to give them a ticket. After a brief conversation, she went away in some distress when they had apparently made it clear to her what she should do with the ticket. Even from four floors up, Seymour had no doubt they were police, Special Branch, what else, the car down on it's suspension with the weight of the two heavies and their weapons. Someone was applying heat, hardly surprising, he thought, in the aftermath of the damn carnage in Castleglen last night. Now he too was caught up in the consequences, the presence of the car below told him so.

The front door intercom buzzed and he pressed the talk button. A dark lyrical male voice with a trace of a Kerry accent, came back through the speaker on his desk,
"It's John Fitzpatrick. I thought you might have a drop of the hard stuff stashed away up there among the interesting files you keep in that office of yours."

"Good evening John, I'm sure your files are much more interesting than mine, but if you're here socially you can come up, by yourself that is, leave your two gorillas outside."

The two cut glasses with their shimmering golden whiskey were on the desk when Fitzpatrick came in, puffing from the exertion of climbing four floors of stairs,
"You can't have too many elderly clients, that's for sure!"

"I make the odd house call."

"So I hear."

The large bulk of Fitzpatrick settled itself in one of the visitor chairs. Seymour raised his glass,
"Your good health."

"Slainte!" came the returned greeting. "For a man of your age, Seymour, you are in remarkably good shape by all accounts."

"It's the stairs you see."

"Oh I'm sure, and a lot more besides."

"Sometimes I get a little work out, but in this business your time is not your own, as you know yourself."

"I don't care for the comparison Seymour, my mother believes her son has a nice steady job defending law and order in this State. You and I may often deal with the same people, but from very different perspectives."

"In theory, John. As you know, the actual situation tends to get a little blurred."

"Not in my book Seymour."

"You must keep more than one book then John, you've used me in the past yourselves, when you didn't want to leave your own clumsy fingerprints all over a problem."

"You have had your uses alright. Whatever about our clumsy fingers, you left your own calling card last evening, I recognized the style. Neat, quick and clean, just like yourself. You know, there's a story about that you could double kick a man so precisely that all he felt was a slight rustle as his trousers brushed up against his balls. I like that Seymour, the precision, the competence, a kind of friendly warning of what you might do."

"Last evening I had a couple of drinks with two nice friends, so I've no idea what you're talking about."

"Of course not, I wouldn't expect anything less from you. Of course the security guard, what's he called, oh yes, McArthur, a bit of a boxer by all accounts, is now sitting up in his hospital bed and very glad to be alive. Last night he was swearing vengeance but to-day, all of a sudden, he just doesn't seem to remember very much at all about the details of last evening. The doctors think it might be late onset concussion. But I've seen it before, how suddenly life looks very good and they don't want to know the details. However, we all know each other in this little country Seymour, as you well know. And in my files you and the late Danny Maguire are associated from way back."

"Now, now John, it's no secret I knew Maguire in London. All that was a very long time ago and you know perfectly well I have had nothing to do with some of his friends here, so don't try to put me in the picture."

"You are in the picture whether you like it or not. I know all about the pair of you in London. Just hear this though, apart from the poor innocent security guard who got killed and I won't even mention the one who is now happily sitting up in his hospital bed, we've had two of our unarmed cops on the receiving end of a grenade. One of them isn't likely to make it, the other, it's for sure he won't see again.

So what I'm saying to you is this, if you know anything about all this or ever find out what the hell went on last night, or anything connected with it that might interest me, you'd better let me in on it."

"Always glad to help John."

"This is a very small fishbowl we all swim in, I generally don't mind your minor unorthodox activities. But this is different, if you have or get anything significant, I want to know."

"As I said, I don't have anything that can help you. My friend Danny Maguire is dead and I'm sorry to lose him. We shared good and bad times when we were young and a couple of Mick's together in London."

"So I have heard."

"But he's dead now, and that's that."

Fitzpatrick finished his drink and stood up,
"I wonder Seymour. It's strange how things can go on, how we can never quite finish with them. Remember what I said and be careful how you go."

"It's always good to see you John, you might take your two associates with you when you leave, I can look after myself."

Fitzpatrick looked back as he opened the office door, "Ah now Seymour, they weren't put there at tax payers expense to keep you healthy, but thanks for the whiskey and remember what I said."

Alone again, Seymour poured himself another whiskey, swirling the soft amber liquid around in the glass, his mind already back to how it had been a long time ago in Sixties London. He moved to a corner of the office, ran the index finger of his left hand down the stack of CD's until he found what he wanted. He turned the volume up and the rock beat hit the walls, bouncing back, demanding life and energy and he could see it all again, the kaleidoscope of bright colours, the pretty girls all long shiny hair, smooth skin and long legs, the clubs, the gambling, the bars, rock and roll on sultry summer nights and freedom and being young and the world was theirs on the wild side of life and the easy money and the hard men and their stories, the fun and the scrapes. Danny Maguire, big, strong and quietly easy with himself. So confidant and his eyes sparkling with mischief.

The rock beat and Mick Jagger's raw, sexy, plaintive voice filled the room as he sang "Street Fighting Man". Seymour lifted the glass and tasted the whiskey. Such a long, long time ago. It was all ended now. Damn it Maguire, he thought, damn it all to hell and he threw the glass at the white wall of his office.

# Chapter 4

After his meeting with Maitland, Tom Ryan felt edgy and depressed, the tiredness starting to creep in on him. The old campus was one of happy memories for him and while he respected Maitland and regarded him as a friend, he was left feeling there was an air of academic unreality about the meeting. And yet he had a sense of foreboding, as though the die was indeed already cast, the script already written and he was following a pre-determined path, going through the motions in a hopeless way. Driving up Leeson Street, heading south from the centre of Dublin to his parents house, he instinctively noticed the two Special Branch men in the parked car, the habit of years. He told himself this was Leeson Street and it was nothing to do with him and continued on.

His parent's house, four miles south of the city centre, was another journey back in time, a reminder of good times and bad, growing up in middle class respectability and security with his younger brother, Jim. Then the traumatic years which were also a part of this house. But the visit to his parents was overdue anyway and would provide some extra cover for his trip to Dublin. In any event, under the circumstances it was as well to see them now, given the uncertain future. He also needed to know where his brother Jim was this weekend.

The big old red brick terraced house was as always, maybe it seemed a little smaller to him these days, but it was essentially immutable. Awakening old associations, bringing him back to his childhood and early teens. The area had changed of course. The city had expanded. A lot of these older houses were now divided into apartments. New people. But the parents held on. Not wanting change. The house becoming slightly more seedy each year that passed. At least they still had each other and were reasonably fit. If he had to disappear for a while, it was going to be difficult. If he was killed...

Again his life was risking bringing trauma into their lives. Life's pattern repeating itself, overlapping. After he had been imprisoned in Northern Ireland, the Irish Government had been embarrassed by the fact that he was the son of one of their senior civil servants. The British papers had had a field day. His father's career had been transplanted into a routine back water as a measure of the displeasure in official circles. The father of one of his comrades had worked for a big building supply firm. Owned by an old southern Anglo-Irish family. After the news of his son being shot dead in the border raid, the father had been fired from his job as foreman. Hard to imagine such things now. But that's the way it had been. The sins of the sons being so blatantly and publicly visited on the fathers. And yet, he felt, it was all about to happen again.

His mother greeted him at the door,
"Ah Tom, how lovely to see you!"

He bent forward and kissed her lightly on the cheek and
noticed how frail she was now,
"Sorry to be so late, but I was up in Dublin visiting Jonathan Maitland in Trinity and thought I'd call by."

"Well indeed, it's lovely to see you anyway, come on in,
your fathers in the front room looking at the television."

"How is he doing after the operation?"

"Well he's coming along, but he really has to take it very
easy now, not that he listens of course!"

She laughed. More memories came back, one of the corner-
stones of childhood, the house filled with her laughing. The
soft bright easy laughing of a young country girl, spilling
out with joy, wanting life to be good. It had stayed with her
through the years. Recently he had started to wonder about
the relationship between his parents, had either one of
them ever wanted someone else? The solidity they had generally provided for their children, contrasted with to-days
turmoil in family life, including his own. There was no going
back to it, but he now appreciated what life had given him.
Perhaps he should have done more with his chances. Things
might have been different.

His father tried to get up when Tom entered the room,
"Tom, good to see you!"
but Tom reached forward and gently pressed his father
back into his comfortable armchair,
"Sit where you are, Dad, I'm just making one of my flying
visits."

His father pressed the mute button and the TV went silent.
How fascinating the pictures became when there was no
sound, just the sudden ticking of the old clock,
"Did I hear you saying to your Mother that you were visiting Professor Maitland?"

Nothing wrong with his hearing anyway,
"Yes Dad, he wanted some background information on a
company he is thinking of approaching to fund a Travelling
Fellowship he wants to set up."

Another small deceit, but there was no alternative he
thought, as he listened to his father's reply,
"What a remarkable man he is. You were so lucky to be
able to study with him for your Masters. You know, sometimes I think you should have stayed in academic life, it
suited you."

"Perhaps, but we all have to find our own path."

When he said it, he wished he hadn't. Talking about his
life's path was not a good idea with his parents. The other

obvious item for conversation, the robbery in his area which now dominated the news as details and speculation gradually emerged, was not on the agenda. When he had been released from prison and had "settled down" his parents hoped that was an end to it. But they knew he had gone North in '69. The subject of politics and the IRA were never discussed again. Tom spoke again,

"Anyway, I should never have said that Trinity could have offered Brendan Behan the Chair of English when they had the chance, that did nothing for my prospects of blending into the Establishment and carving out an academic career!"

"No, I can imagine that! Even Trinity with its broad horizons would have had problems accommodating the bold Brendan, God rest him. I really can't see him in front of a class. He'd either be stupefied with drink or singing his IRA songs", his father replied laughing at the notion.

"Well, he wouldn't have been the first academic to leave something to be desired in his behaviour, inside class or outside, but with him at least they would have had the prospect of something worthwhile and original being produced. Anyway, even my floating the notion was too rich for them and that was that. Obviously I didn't have the proper respect for the academic niceties."

Tom turned to his mother as she appeared with a tea tray, swearing to himself that he shouldn't have come when he was so tired,

"Tell me, do you know if Jim is at home this week, I was thinking of giving him a call?"

"No, himself and Ellen are in Hawaii this weekend and all next week. The annual sales conference is on. Not that he'll have much time for Hawaii from what he tells me. He really works far too hard."

His fathers voice came in, strong with enthusiasm,
"But hasn't he made a great career for himself. When you think of that beautiful house they have in California. It's out of this world."

Then his mother,
"And of course, you've made a great career too, Tom."

Just a little too late to dispel the implied comparison and touch of disappointment. He knew they were both good people, trying to do their best in a world which was so different from the one they had known when young. He wondered how they viewed their family in such changed times. He also felt responsible for the major stresses in their life, it was a permanent barrier, always between them,
"Well not much point phoning him in California, I'd end up talking to the Mexican maid or the kids. Not sure which is the more difficult!"

That took the sting out of the air and they all laughed at the idea of this phone call.

His mother chimed in,

"Well the children are complete Americans, of course, but they are lovely in their own way. I just wish we would see more of them. Since they've grown up they really don't want to come over here like they used to."

He thought about it for a moment, then said,

"I might get over to the States for a while myself in the next few weeks, possibly even before Christmas. A friend of mine wants me to go and I've been putting it off. And there are some contacts I need to make with the New York office. I'll give Jim a call, who knows, maybe I can spend Christmas with them in California."

Might as well keep the worst from them for as long as possible.

"By the way, do you know where they are staying in Hawaii?"

His mother answered,

"I'm sure they said they would be at the Hilton. Sure he usually stays at a Hilton anyway, wherever he is!"

No doubt there would be several Hiltons in Hawaii, but it was enough information to allow him find Jim without too much trouble.

After he left, the house was silent as his mother and father each thought their own thoughts for a while. The suddenness of the visit, the tired, troubled look he had about him, the news of the terrible events in Castleglen, all this worried them. Something was surely wrong. Dear God, his mother wondered, what had happened to him now, this wayward son of hers with no sense, reminding her of herself in so many ways? Was it work, this love affair with Kara, was it his ex-wife Hazel or was it the IRA? They could only wait to find out and keep hoping that whatever it was, it was not the IRA again. Surely the cease-fire would mean it couldn't be the IRA? They could only hope so.

# Chapter 5

Late Friday night in Castleglen and Noreen Doyle was sitting squashed in a corner in the crowded pub, beside her date for the evening, O'Sullivan. She uncrossed her legs and wriggled slightly as she pulled her short black skirt down over her legs and with two quick movements brushed away an imaginary speck of dust from the skirt. In the movement of her hand, her carefully painted bright red fingernails flashed and sparkled. The colour of her nails matched the red polo necked sweater she had chosen to wear with the skirt. She had taken such trouble to look good and he'd said nothing. She kept hoping things would improve, but it was not going to be a successful evening, she knew that now.

It was getting late now, the pub would close soon. They had been there for almost two hours now, no, she had been there for two hours, he had been there for an hour and a half. She didn't like waiting in pubs on her own. He was always late, had been on each of their two previous dates anyway, but this was the worst yet.

She sipped her gin and tonic, not really liking the taste and looked around again at the boisterous crowd. Then she turned her head to look at him. He was just as he had been five minutes before, staring absently into his glass of bright yellow orange juice into which the ice had long melted. She looked away; it would be time to go soon.

Well, on the plus side, he was different, you had to admit that at least. Certainly a change from that bastard Farrell. The girls at the office had told her all about Farrell, afterwards. Still, at least Farrell looked like something and took the trouble to dress himself to look like something. O'Sullivan looked scruffy in his sweater and jeans, not that she'd ever seen him in anything else. She wondered what he would look like in a suit and tie. Surely he must have a suit and tie. He looked like he could have been a farm labourer, even his fingernails were dirty. How did he get into such a state with his job as Head of the Social Security Office in the town, but then she realized she knew little about him and his life anyway. Perhaps he was married, well you never knew, he could have a wife and family up North for all she or anyone else knew. Maybe he was queer? No, that didn't seem likely, they were all careful about how they looked, she knew that. But why was he always asking her about Tom Ryan, you'd think she was having an affair with Ryan the way he went on. To-night he wanted to know where Ryan was. How the hell did he think she'd know where Ryan was on his weekends? If he'd wanted to know Ryan's salary and which bank it was paid into, that she could have told him. Who were his friends, where did he go to, you'd think she was in Personnel not Accounts. Then after all the questions about Ryan, he'd gone silent and morose on her.

Men, they had no idea. She should apply for a transfer to head office in Dublin before it was too late, this small town was getting her down. She uncrossed and re-crossed her legs, pushing her thigh tighter against his. No response. She took up her drink again. Suddenly he got up and started speaking to her. He seemed agitated, excited, and she had trouble following what he was saying with the strong accent. Something about having to go home now and make an urgent phone call. For the love of Jesus, she thought, getting up to go and pulling her skirt down again.

# Chapter 6

The phone rang, interrupting her thoughts, and Kara walked across the room to answer it. It was Tom Ryan telling her he was back in his car and leaving his parents house. He would be with her in about twenty minutes. She told him she was looking forward to seeing him and to be careful driving and that she loved him.

Apart from the woman, there was nothing Japanese about the room. She was sitting on a large, soft sofa, which was covered with a big floral pattern against a white background. The sofa ran at right angles away from the two floor-to-ceiling Georgian windows that looked out over Dublin Bay. In the centre of the room a chandelier hung from the ornately worked ceiling rose, its dimmed lights giving a warm diffuse glow in the room. In front of the sofa was a large, square, glass topped coffee table with square chromed legs. The apartment was on the third floor in one of a terrace of expensive older houses that faced the sea on the south side of Dublin. The pretty, petite Japanese woman did not seem at all out of place in the mixture of old and new styles in the apartment, perhaps because she had chosen the furniture and fittings herself shortly after she came to Dublin in 1982.

Kara sat back on her sofa and her thoughts returned to the

fax she had received from Tokyo that morning. It was from Bansan, the businessman she had met on the Tokyo — Paris flight when she first left Japan. The contents of the fax told her of Bansan's developing plans for the future and brought nearer the prospect of having to face a conflict in her life. But that was in the future, she didn't have to face it now, no decision was necessary now, her life could go on as it had.

*   *   *

By the time the 747 touched down in Paris in August of 1982, she had already decided to go to bed with the passenger she sat beside on the long flight. He had asked her why she was going to Ireland, she told him it was as far away from Japan as possible and she thought it was a totally different place. He had never been there he said. Neither had she, she told him, but she was seeking a complete, total change in her life and that was why she was going there. It was not that Bansan was physically attractive, she didn't find him so, but he was obviously a man of influence and power. These were qualities that were always attractive to her, perhaps particularly now that she was just divorced and on her way to a new and uncertain life. As she thought about it now all these years later, she understood that she was feeling insecure at that time, both as a woman and in terms of what the total change she had undertaken would mean for her. In any event, and for whatever complex mixture of reasons, she had decided her onward connection from Paris to Dublin could wait a little longer than she had originally planned. In Paris she would start to claim her own independence, her own sexual power. She was almost 38 years old, but her good looks attracted men and she would retain this to the envy and jealousy of other women.

That night, in his five star hotel suite on the Rue de Rivoli, the sex was functional. Bansan, interesting to talk with, a man of much knowledge and many secrets, like a Japanese warrior, moving between continents as he pursued his objectives. But physically ugly, a useless and crude lover, without charm or passion. Her description of it afterwards used the English word "disaster". But it served its purpose. Bansan was to be useful to her in the unfolding events of her new life.

She spent the next five days with him in Paris. While he attended his business meetings, she was free to explore the city as it baked dry and dusty in the scorching still heat of the long summer days, its wide streets and boulevards left to the tourists by most of the inhabitants who had fled to the seaside. She delighted in exploring its museums, art galleries, beautiful buildings, large public squares and gardens. At an exhibition she saw Renoir's painting, "Two Sisters on a Terrace". She had stood transfixed by the delicate portrayal of two girls, both young, but of different ages.

One still a child, the other becoming a young woman, becoming aware of herself as a complex sexual being, turning away from the things of childhood. As Kara stood in the cool stillness and echoing silence of the gallery, the captured portrayal of wistful beauty, the different feelings of hope and promise as shown in the two young girls in early life, overcame her and she felt warm tears flow uncontrollably down her face. Now she wondered why she had cried then, what was it that had happened to her in seeing this picture.

She was brought back abruptly to the present by the sound of the doorbell ringing and Tom Ryan using his key to enter the apartment. She looked at herself in the mirror, and confirmed to herself that time had treated her kindly; she still looked beautiful, her face belying her years. Turning she smiled to greet him. She thought he looked tired, but didn't say so.

*     *     *

As he opened the door, Tom heard the music start and the sound spilled out of the apartment bringing to him the gentle lilting voice of Fats Domino singing "I Want To Walk You Home". Kara came forward to greet him, smiling and moving rhythmically to the music. Surrounded by the mellow loving tones of Fats Domino, she looked wonderful and her easy, graceful, sassy movements to the music entranced him. He felt so tired and worn, she looked so alive. It seemed to him to be a moment of pure escapist, dreamy magic set in life's meaningless harsh rush and taking him away from his own frightening problems. She gently pulled away from him, telling him to sit down and she would get some food for him.

He was now very tired but restless, so he went over to the windows and looked out at the lights across the bay. The apartment had a view right across the bay to Howth, the outline of the bay etched against the night by the curving string of bright dots formed by the distant streetlights. He could see the alternate flashes of the Bailey and the Kish lighthouses. Peaceful and regular. His thoughts ran on from earlier that night, the old University buildings and grounds set like an island of tranquillity in the heart of Dublin city and of Maitland talking about Joyce. He looked out now at the lighthouses, seemingly timeless as they sent out their dependable sweeping bright beams of light across the sea, just the way they had in the time of Joyce's "Ulysses". As he looked across the bay at the outline of Howth Head his mind wandered to Molly Bloom and her erotic soliloquy back in her bed in the city. This old house, before it's conversion into modern apartments, would have rung to the songs of that period. Songs which needed beautiful period drawing rooms with high elegant ceilings, Moore's Melodies, tunes from operettas and from the Victorian Music

Halls. The time between 1900 and the First World War must have been one of considerable prosperity and stability in Dublin and elsewhere in Britain and much of the rest of the British Empire. But Ireland had declined economically, the price of the revolution perhaps. The passage of time, the transitory nature of this life and his own possible imminent death combined to play on his mind through his tiredness and seemed to heighten the intensity of the overwhelming desire he felt for Kara. How easy it was to love her. How crazy it was to love her, the complications. He sighed, that was the trouble with falling in love again late in life, there were always complications from both your pasts. Perhaps everyone should fall in love just once. It would be a lot simpler.

She came back into the room, all bright and breezy, "Now my big Irishman, I have some Sushi for you and Miso soup to start. And since you are a mere Geyshing, I also ordered your favourite desert, "Banana Tropicana" and of course, I have some Kirin beer for you."

She smiled. He put his arms around her and drew her to him. Her soft body folded into his and she smiled up at him. It was always the same. He couldn't touch her without being aroused. He found her totally erotic. Ridiculous, how a woman of her age could look so beautiful, be so irresistible.

\*　　\*　　\*

As she felt his strong arms enfold her she nestled into him. It was good to be with him, feel his large strong body hold her. She knew he was crazy about her and she believed that she also loved him. But love followed by commitment was something she didn't want. It was not a part of her life anymore. Not with anyone since leaving the man she had married. There had been too many lovers anyway. Some she cared about, others she knew were just to break periods of loneliness, others were useful to her. Now she found she was caught between conflicting emotions. It was becoming increasingly hard to maintain her Japanese view of life, that it could be separated into compartments which didn't interfere with each other. In particular to contain the problem of falling in love with Tom Ryan. Yet she knew she wanted him. She glowed in the power of his love, coming alive again, the joy of being wanted beyond reason. The wild passion of their lovemaking. She gently eased herself away from him,

"Come and eat now, Mr. Irishman."

She set out the meal for him and told him she had eaten already,

"So Ry-san, what's new?"

She was aware that somehow he was involved with the IRA, but he never went into detail. She knew about his being captured at seventeen and imprisoned. Now as he ate, he told her he had a problem and would have to get out of the country for a while. She assumed it was to avoid the police,

"Is there anything I can do?"

"No. All you have to do is love me!"

She smiled back at him and took his hand and they went to her bedroom. He watched her as she undressed. The small brown body. To his loving eyes, she could at the same time look both comical and erotic. As she undressed, she made funny little movements, conscious that he was looking at her. As always, it made him smile with amusement and delight as he watched her apply her beauty oils to her face and then theatrically look at him and pat her face and neck to complete her beauty treatment. Moments of delay and anticipation, looking at each other, enjoying each others presence, being alone and quiet before they made love.

Her soft childlike body contrasted against the white sheets on the bed. He put his hand gently against her cheek and looked into her face. Her warm brown eyes looked back into his, unblinking. His heart ached for her, his whole being wanted her. In the silence of the room as he could feel his heart beat out it's claim on life, he realized his entire existence now revolved around her. He put his hand down between her legs. She was soaking wet.

She gently pulled him on top of her and he entered her. They started to make love with an easy naturalness, with her it was always so simple. He looked down at her parted lips, she looked like she was just sixteen. Her fingers dug into him and the demanding urgency of their desire for each other as their bodies sought each other, became the only thing that mattered and in the frantic seeking they became one, losing themselves in each other. She came with short gasps of pleasure and she bit into his shoulder. As she subsided and relaxed, she smiled up at him and said "Kimouchi" and they gently laughed together.

They fell asleep, he with his hand between her legs, she holding him. He woke in a little while and wanted her again. They made love again in the dishevelled bed and the room full of the smell of their earlier lovemaking and the stickiness of the bedclothes. The prospect of death brought everything in life into an even sharper more vivid reality, he wanted to taste life, grasp the sensuality of her body for as long as possible. All the wild desires inside him released into her. All the unfulfilled longings. Escaping the lonely isolation and damnation of unsure individual existence into the hot melting desire of being with and in her with no limits, each totally exposed to the others raw emotion, urgent wants and then erupting release. His entire body shook for minutes afterwards as she held him gasping for air, the longings of his whole soul having poured out of him. Echoes of aching desires beyond words, without description, coming from some ancient pre-existence carrying him out of this world into another only ever vaguely perceived in this haunted escape of the soul.

As his breathing and heart rate returned to normal and the world came back into focus, he lay beside her and looked at her and held her and thought of this wondrous journey she took him on in their lovemaking. How it was unlike anything he had ever experienced. He remembered when they had first become lovers, she used to say to him "Nothing lasts". He understood the cautious warning message she was sending him. How this was her experience and indeed his own, but he didn't want to hear it.

As he drifted into sleep again he realized that her statement could be all too true and all too soon. This life is a very temporary thing, precarious at the best of times, no one knows what's coming next. For him it could end very soon, the spectre of violent death hung over him. But he wanted life, wanted her, he was determined to find a way out. He wanted this to last, believing they had found something entirely special and valuable. Like nothing before. He must get out of the IRA, he wanted to live with her. Now that he had found her, he couldn't let her go. Wanted the taste and the erotic experience of her, the runaway freedom to lose himself with and in her. To escape mortality and lose himself in the wonder that he saw as her.

# Chapter 7

It was almost 6am and still dark night on Monday morning as Tom Ryan drove out of Dublin heading west for Castleglen. It had been a bittersweet week-end. She seemed to take the news of his plan well, it was sometimes hard to know what she thought, but no doubt if you had grown up in Japan immediately after the war, you were likely to be stoical. The early morning news on the car radio had shifted the robbery of last week to the third news item of the morning as the world turned its attention to other events. For Ryan it was going to change his life.

As usual his boss was already working at his desk at 8am, trying to get the more important decisions made before the merry-go-round of phones and meetings got under way. Ryan knocked on Duggan's half open door and was told to come in.

Though the two men were never very close, Duggan had helped Tom get the job with the Authority. Duggan admired the way Ryan had sorted himself out after his foolish adventure with the IRA as a youngster. Being of the same generation and background, it was more than just understanding, more a case of "there but for the grace of God go I". And Ryan had worked hard for his two degrees.

He worked hard for the Authority as well. It was too bad that his marriage to Hazel had broken up. But these things happen. There was a lot of pressure these days.

"Hello Michael, can you spare me a few minutes?"

"No problem Tom, sit down. How are things?"

"Well I wanted to see you about taking some time off. I saw my doctor over the weekend and had a chat with him. You know, after Hazel and I broke up, it was a very difficult period for me. I started to hit the bottle rather too hard."

Duggan looked more closely at Ryan, he hadn't noticed it before, but Ryan did indeed look the worse for wear, "You wouldn't be the first to do that, but I must say, you kept it under control as far as anyone here knew!"

Duggan thought he had heard something about spending romantic weekends in Dublin. He wondered if perhaps that had gone wrong too.

"Yes, you're right Michael, the drinking never got entirely out of control, at least not so far, but the doctor has suggested I do something about it, apparently my liver isn't what it should be. So I've decided to turn myself in for treatment, with Christmas coming up the doc thinks I should go now. It may take some weeks, they won't say exactly how long they need to straighten me out. But with Christmas, I thought, if it was OK with you, I might take the following few weeks as my annual leave? I'd prefer it that way so it needn't be officially recorded by Personnel as a problem."

Odd though, he had never thought Ryan was the type to let alcohol get the better of him, but you never knew, "I see. How are things in your section at the moment?"

"Pretty good. It's been quiet since the last big project went through and the ones we have right now are at an early stage. Shouldn't be a problem if I'm not here for a little while."

"Well, under the circumstances, you'd better go ahead and take the medical advice. We've enough people in trouble with alcohol in the Authority as it is! You get yourself sorted out, I'm sure you can do it. In any event we can't afford to risk losing you to the drink. When do you think you would like to start?"

"If it's OK with you, I'd like to go more or less right away?"

His secretary met him on the way back to his own office, "Tom, there you are, there's a call for you, personal, will you take it in your office?"

He was pretty sure he knew who it would be.

"Ryan."

The unmistakable accent of O'Sullivan came down the line to him,

"I was trying to reach you all weekend, we've got the preliminary forensic report. There is no item listed which would suggest the boys had the holdall in the Ford. No remains of metal parts, zip fasteners, banknotes or anything else. That means they must have left it at the drop site. Just like I said."

"I see. I had to go to Dublin this weekend and I'm tied up here with meetings all day. I'll go out there this evening and see what I can find. There is another drop site in the area that we sometimes use. I'll check it."

"You'd better do that. I'll be in touch with you to-night. Make sure you're in."

"Don't contact me at home, I can't be sure the phone is safe. Call me here to-morrow morning."

"You don't seem to understand, I'm coming round to your place to-night, this can't wait. I'll be there at eleven, just make sure you're in. One other piece of information from our little girl in Forensics, Jones was shot in the head, at close range from the front, in the car, with Maguire's gun."

"I see."

After the phone call, Ryan tried to pace himself as he continued to put the pieces of his plan in place. First he talked briefly with his immediate work group, saying he was to be away unexpectedly for a few weeks, vaguely suggesting he was taking some time to sort out a personal matter. Then they discussed the various projects they were each working on. Afterwards, talking between themselves, they were all a little surprised, but then Christmas/ New Year was a time when many people took leave. He was a hard worker, they were all sure he could use the break.

On his way through reception, he asked Joan if she remembered the call he had first thing that morning and told her that if the same man called again to just say he was out of the office. Joan smiled, blushed and said she would. By 10.00am he was in his car driving fast for Shannon Airport. He just made the New York flight.

# Chapter 8

When Tom had phoned from New York, using the street pay phone and reversing the charges to Hawaii, he had effectively invited himself for Christmas. That was a surprise, but it was OK with Ellen, she had a soft spot for Tom. He had a slightly dreamy quality about him, not like Jim. Jim was always pragmatic, a realist. His was a matter of fact approach to life. Problems were there to be solved. If there was no solution to a problem you lived with it and went on to solve a different problem. Life lived by the problem solving methods of science. Jim was solid, capable, always punctual, entered fully into the American way of life and business and relished it. Life was an opportunity. You expended energy, were smart and got ahead. Ellen knew he would always take care of the family. She enjoyed what America had brought them. Their lifestyle, the feeling of progress.

But this dreamy brother, with his wider interests, feeling for life, the romantic a little wild, brought a new different welcome dimension. There was something irresistible, exciting in a forbidden way, about his taking up arms at seventeen. A man who would push things to extremes, risk everything, life itself, for an idea. Ellen took a delight in her kids, Kevin and Jean, but they were busy with their own lives now. Jim was always busy. She liked having Tom around. Since he had free time in the period before Christmas, she took him shopping with her for new clothes. In and out of the changing rooms she stepped, showing off another dress. Turning, showing how it looked this way and that, showing how it fitted here, how it moved as she moved, smiling and waiting for his comments. It was flirtatious, a come on, a kind of courtship ritual, forbidden and fun.

*     *     *

Jim had been more than just surprised when Tom phoned to say he wanted to spend Christmas with them. He didn't discuss his feelings of unease with Ellen, but he felt sure there was something going on. This wasn't quite normal, too sudden. Sure it had happened before, the Christmas after Tom and Hazel split up. But that was different. He thought Tom had sorted himself out now and Jim knew there was Kara. The great romantic was in love again. But maybe the Japanese love affair had come to an end. Being Tom, that could have caused problems. Damn fool. Women weren't to be taken so seriously. Romance, ridiculous if you were over sixteen. Life was practical and tough. No place for such foolish feelings. They only caused trouble.

On Saturday, December 24, Christmas Eve, the entire Ryan family together with Tom went to Mid-Night Mass in the exquisite local church. Ultra modern, clean crisp lines, full of the beautiful people, beautiful singing, celebrating the coming of the Saviour. Not that any of the Ryan's, or perhaps even most of the congregation, regarded themselves as Catholics, but Christmas was special. In any event, Jim believed that you needed some kind of group identity and with the kids education they had always had some association with the Church. The devil you knew was best. Not that there was too much resemblance with the Catholic Church at home. This was California after all.

Afterwards, Tom and Jim sat up late talking, Jim with a glass of Kentucky Bourbon, Tom with his Irish Whiskey. A Christmas tree with the expensive presents under it, the big room lit by candlelight that cast shadows and softened the bright splashes of colour in the room. The two brothers had always talked easily with each other while growing up, at least until Tom ended up in jail at seventeen. There was a bond of closeness between them that survived their differing natures and interests. To an extent, each could see the inner workings of the other, see the differences, understand how and why each was driven. Even when they disagreed about life, there was still an empathy for each others point of view by knowing how and why it had been formed, what mattered to each of them and why. It was like they were twins, but not the same, opposite and complimentary, coming back together from a shared past.

That Christmas night, Jim was relaxed and in expansive mood. Enjoying having Tom here, enjoying the feeling of home and Christmas. The warm sounds of jazz coming out of the stereo system. For Tom, it was like he had entered an island of peace, having left one island just in time to escape the inferno which would overrun his life there, he now had a moment in life to enjoy normality again, briefly before the inferno jumped after him and forced him on again. He tried to put the immediate dangers out of his mind, tried to relax and absorb the healing atmosphere of this beautiful comfortable room, enjoy the moment, "Who's playing?" Tom asked.

"That's Ben Webster, probably the sax players all time favourite tenor sax player. He plays like an angel. His personal life was an awful mess. He was an alcoholic and one of the stories about him is that he threw a woman out of a third floor hotel window and had to leave town fast. But he plays saxophone with such expression and delicate feeling, his playing is incredible. Perhaps I should describe him as a fallen angel! I suppose in life generally, the fallen angels are more interesting!"

"Yes, maybe so."

"I imagine, like Ben Webster, they are a pain in the neck to have around too long or if you have to live with them, but they make life interesting!"

They were both getting drunk, they both laughed and Jim continued,

"You know playing the saxophone is very much like making love. All the basic ingredients are much the same. For either process to go right, you have to be relaxed and you have to have energy, you must know what you are doing and like it, the instrument and you have to be warmed up and wet and you must play like you and the instrument are one and the same thing!"

"I suppose that pretty much makes the comparison all right! Since you don't make it in the fallen angels stakes, do you have any time to play your own sax these days?"

"No, I haven't played for years. You see unfortunately the analogy with women continues, if you don't play the sax regularly, she will screech at you and refuse to play at all! You know Tom, still on the subject of sex, I was thinking the other day, the whole damn problem in Northern Ireland is really about sex and the lack of it!"

The Northern problem was a dangerous subject between them and Tom certainly didn't want it raised to-night, but this unusual view of the North brought a burst of laughter from him,

"OK, I haven't heard that one before, so go on!"

"Yeah, you see all the others who came to Ireland, you

know the Celts, the Vikings, the Danes, the English, well sure for a while they just married each other, fought off the local inhabitants and continued with the plunder bit. But then they eventually had a few jars in the local pub, fancied a young one and got hitched. So sex with a little help from the drink made the whole lot into just one more or less homogeneous group. Now, now this isn't as crazy as you might think. We all know the English had awful trouble with their representatives going native and had to keep sending over fresh supplies of proper Englishmen to re-instil discipline and keep up proper standards in Church and State."

Tom thought that he probably knew a lot more about the historical background than Jim, but Jim obviously had something he wanted to say and this wasn't the time to stop him in full flight, perhaps the cease-fire made it a lighter subject than usual, even for Jim,
"OK, so tell me all about the North and your new theory!"

"Ah well, that little lot of lower class Scottish Presbyterians who were given the land 400 years ago in reward for their fighting for the English armies, had been told how much better they were than the locals and the damn fools stub-bornly continued to believe it. So they didn't go down to the pub and have a few jars with the locals. They kept to themselves and didn't mix. Lack of sexual drive, no freeing of their Calvinist inhibitions. That's what did it. And you see, it's a problem that can't be solved. The gene mix they came with is set forever. They'll never change. They will always be separate. The homogenization process never got a chance with them. Funny when you think of all the peoples who were homogenized in Ireland. But not them."

"Your genetic theory doesn't sound too hopeful Jim. Based on your theory, we are doomed to continue with this problem forever."

"Well perhaps not. The planet is now becoming such a mess, that we have a real chance of wiping out all human life before long. That would solve your local Northern Ireland problem."

"Your new theories are sounding even more gloomy, but maybe that's the only way of solving it."

Tom was happy to move off the subject of Northern Ireland, it was dangerously close to his having to reveal his reasons for being in California this Christmas. He welcomed the chance to get Jim onto an alternative subject, "So, from a scientific point of view, how long do you think we have to wait?"

"Perhaps only 50 years, perhaps 100 years. I don't think you'll have to wait longer than that from what I see."

"Sounds great for the Northern problem, but not too optimistic for humanity in general."

"No, I have to say it's difficult to be overly optimistic. The problem is that there is no mechanism that I can see which will allow the necessary action to be taken to reverse the problems being generated in the modern world. In the last 100 years, we have done some marvellous things through technology to make life much more convenient for most of us. But these have been cheap tricks of technology and we haven't understood the problems they are causing until too late. But the economic demand is for cheap tricks, there is no economic or political correction mechanism for the long term problems."

"But Jim, you make your money from technology. Without technology you don't have a job."

"That's true. Specifically I make my money by supplying the Chemical, Pharmaceutical and related industries with technology. But you know, I sometimes think that Chemistry should be banned, outlawed as a crime against humanity. The only problem with that is that it is only the Chemists who can fix the mess they have helped create. And now we have the biological sciences playing God with Genetic Engineering and all the hype is full of the same "no risk and something for nothing" promises that were made about Atomic Power in the Fifties."

"You sound extraordinarily disillusioned with Science."

"I suppose I am really. Science has misrepresented itself. It appears to have come up with "explanations" about Life and the Universe, but in reality, Science is great at explaining one thing by saying it's like another. That does nothing to provide a real explanation for anything. And on the technology side, we are really just doing cheap tricks which have long term problems we can't solve."

"Jim, you are beginning to sound like a Bishop who has just announced he doesn't believe in God anymore!"

"Probably more scientists than Bishops believe in God these days!"

"Perhaps we had better call it a night on that! For a couple of atheists it's a strangely appropriate conversation for Christmas Eve, bringing us back to the idea of God!"

They laughed, got up and hugged each other and wished each other a Happy Christmas. The conversation had gone off in an odd direction. Tom still hadn't said why he was here. That was the way he wanted it, it would wait, no need to spoil Christmas. For now it was enough that he was here in California with Jim and Ellen, the kids, Kevin and Jean. Enjoying a family Christmas, peaceful and secure. His thoughts turned to Hazel, his ex-wife. Perhaps it was inevitable, Christmas always brought back such memories, memories of family and how it had been at other times. They had had so many Christmas's together. He wondered how this Christmas was for her. Then he thought of Kara and wished he could be with her now.

After Tom had left the room, Jim picked up the phone, dialled a number in Ireland, his cheerfulness lost now as the alcohol kicked in, exaggerating the solitary feeling, connecting him back again, things that might have been. Her sleepy voice answered and he wished Hazel a happy Christmas, just like he always did.

# Chapter 9

O'Sullivan had no trouble finding her. She still went by the name Mrs. Ryan, Mrs. Hazel Ryan. She saw no reason to change it. Despite the bitterness she felt, even still all these years later, it seemed proper, correct. She was still Mrs. Ryan. Still living in the old cottage she and Tom had renovated together. Her bank account, telephone, all her personal matters were in that name. Why would she change it? The Judicial Separation was just that, it wasn't divorce. Maybe when divorce became available in Ireland, if ever, she would divorce him, perhaps. She knew about his subsequent love affairs, had heard about his latest flame, that Japanese bitch, even seen them together in Dublin. How could he? It was disgusting. Making a fool of himself again, with her. Just like Tom bloody Ryan. He never had any sense.

It was the afternoon of the first Saturday in the New Year, January 1, 1995, when that miserable creep O'Sullivan called around to see her and started her mind down the long avenue to the past. She had spent the Christmas/ New Year holiday with her parents in Dublin before coming back to the stone cottage she and Tom had bought when they were together. The holiday period had yet again been

filled with awkward silences and inexpressible views, a continuing commentary of failed communications, unbridge-
able gulfs, lack of understanding. Lack of respect really. All
compounded by her marriage to Tom Ryan of course, but
really reflecting deeper problems. And none of it sub-
sequently undone in her parent's eyes by the eventual failure of the marriage. She knew that there was no use in
talking, any attempts to form a basis of understanding only
served to heighten the lack of understanding, causing
further frustration and irritation between her and her parents. So the problems were no longer discussed, her reality,
her needs, distanced her from them. Coming back to the
old cottage, her former home with Tom, just completed the
depressing circle she found enclosing her at the beginning
of this new year.

She thought how she had been a nice, uncomplicated, Protestant schoolgirl when she met him. She was just fifteen, he
was almost seventeen. At a rugby club dance. Tall, skinny
and serious he was, with a determined look about him.
Good looking too, interested in literature. He asked her
what she was reading. It was all very innocent. A few stolen
kisses, going to a film together, loving goodnight embraces,
all romantic, her first real crush. His too. She had broken
the taboo, gone with a Catholic. Not told her parents about
him. He hadn't told her about the IRA. She found out
through the newspapers and the radio when he was

arrested in the North. Her parents found out when they discovered her crying in her room.

His parents knew nothing about her until she arrived at the door of their solid red-bricked terraced house two days later. Having taken her courage, she would not deny him. She loved him. His parents were already in a state of shock, their lives in turmoil, out of control. The father looked at her as though she was mad. But the mother had put her arms around her and held her and told her it would be alright, somehow it would be alright. That she was glad she had come. Of course, his mother had noticed the school uniform, a Protestant school uniform, and the name, Hazel, but it didn't matter, certainly not in the midst of all that trauma. It was the least of his mother's worries. It takes a big problem to put a small one in perspective. The notion of love, love of Tom was all too welcome in that cold fearful climate that now inhabited the Ryan household. His mother brought her into the big old fashioned kitchen with the black tile floor and made her tea and gave her some of her home made cake. And then held her again as she cried again for Tom and the awful trouble they were in.

Jim had come in and seen her crying, with his mother holding her and patting her gently and saying,

"There, there now, it'll be all right, don't worry now child."

Jim. She and he were thrown together in the loss of Tom.

She could talk to him about Tom, hear him explain, tell her
things she didn't already know. They were friends together,
in the endlessness of the long young years while Tom was
in prison. His prison sentence when she first heard it
seemed to her at fifteen like an eternity. Two years later,
on one hot summers day when she would have been just
seventeen, Jim sixteen, they had taken a walk together in
the Dublin Mountains and friendship turned to love.

It wasn't right, they knew that, but they couldn't help it,
they wanted each other with all the single minded, inexperi-
enced desire of being young. Intensified perhaps by a
shared feeling of loss? A secret, no one must know. They
continued to make their periodic visits to Tom in his Belfast
prison, but she went separately now, not when Jim went.
She was afraid that Tom would notice, sense the love
between Jim and her.

They knew a month in advance of his being released, that
he was coming out of jail. He had served five years and
was now to be released early with his remission for good
behaviour. She told Jim that they would, could, no longer
be lovers. She couldn't do this to Tom. She knew Jim was
being torn apart as he pleaded with her. No, they had to
stop.

She told Tom she had had an affair, a brief affair of no
importance, while he was in prison. Yes, it was all over

now, finished, she was sorry, but it didn't mean anything. She knew that hurt him, the idea of her making love to someone else, that it hadn't been him who was her first and only love. That he thought "How could she?" That he had tried to be sensible. Shake it off, put it in perspective, believe it hadn't been important. But she also knew he wondered. Believed the first time was surely always important. Yes, of course he accepted she was lonely. But, and there always was a but.

Perhaps she should never have told him anything. What difference would it have made? It might have helped. The first hurting avoided, a better, simpler start to their married life. The storybook romance, waiting for your young love to be released from prison. A man who had fought for his principles, risked death, paid the price. All romantic and true. But perhaps that was what was needed when you are very young, the romantic ideal. Anything else is second best, difficult to take. Flawed and maybe even containing the seeds of it's own destruction.

But there were other factors. He came out of prison, quiet and mature, older than his years, touched with the sadness of life already. Guilty about the problems he had brought on the family. Determined to sort himself out, keep a low profile, try to redeem himself somehow. Working nights after his teaching job to complete the Masters degree he did in Trinity. Money always tight. Her parents were totally opposed to the marriage. She wondered why she and Tom hadn't emigrated, got the hell out of Ireland, made a fresh start. Too late now. What if she'd stayed with Jim, it would have been different she was sure. Jim had sense. He had got out and made a life for himself.

It was always so awkward, when they met again. Him with Ellen, she with Tom. What were they supposed to be, friends? What a ridiculous word, how could you move from lover to friend? They would catch each other's eye across a room sometimes, perhaps each of them at that moment thinking of the past, what might have been. Sometimes end up standing close to each other, aware of the others body, close, but untouchable. What the hell was love anyway? The opposite side of the coin from hate, love turns inevitably to hate? Did she hate Jim? No. Did that mean she didn't love him? Did she hate Tom? Yes. Did that mean she loved him? She thought she wasn't sure what love was anymore.

She wondered what had made her marry Tom? Loyalty, not wishing to let him down after all those years in prison? Encouraged to do it to spite her parent's dire warnings. Stubbornly driven to keep to the original idea? All of those things.

It had been a mistake of course. Now she couldn't help but blame Tom, for him she had given up everything, it was his fault it didn't work. She would now never forgive him. He never appreciated it, what she had sacrificed for him. Giving up her love of Jim. Funny how you didn't remember the grand passions of sex, just the odd times, the shared moments, being together on a bus, a look, laughing together.

Then that creep, O'Sullivan coming around. At first she thought he was just another of the hunting pack of foxes. Looking for an easy conquest now that she was alone. But no, not that one, he was single-minded, ambitious, driven. A truly devious little bastard. There was something sinister about his contacting her, asking where Tom might be. Perhaps it was because his visit was so totally unexpected or his arriving while she was still stressed out after spending Christmas with her parents, but when O'Sullivan had asked her where Tom might be, she first said she had no idea but then she had said he might be with his brother in California. Or maybe it wasn't the stress, just some moment of evil from her unconscious mind, telling her not to give a damn, Tom Ryan was no longer her concern, why should she be protective of his whereabouts anymore. Dear God, what a life. She had given up so much, obtained so little. To be brought back to her dreams of what might have been. And now Tom going around with that Oriental bitch.

She thought of Jim again, how it had been and remembered the poem "Reflexions",

*Red wine and firelight*
*The first delicious sip and you come alive*
*And sip by sip the sweet taste captures you*

*The flames rise and warm*
*And the heat grows*
*Filling the room with brightness and colour*

*But the wine is finished*
*And leaves only a dull confusion*
*It's over*

*And the flames die*
*And leave only cold and dirty ashes*
*It's over*

*After all, it was just an interlude*
*The light and heat and sweetness*
*Transient in a bitter, cold darkness*

She started to cry, grief turned to despair and she was left sobbing her heart out, alone in the cottage.

# Chapter 10

Neither Ellen nor Jim had asked Tom how long he was staying, they assumed he was taking the usual long Christmas/ New Year break that all of Europe seemed to enjoy these days. The time passed quickly with parties in the elaborate homes of friends and New Years Eve in the even more elaborate home of Jim's boss, J Aldrich Parker, President of the international Parker-Wotton Corporation. A sparkling occasion, with a six piece band playing and professional catering. Jim, Ellen and Tom together with the other revellers welcomed the New Year, 1995, and wished each other well. In that glittering happy crowd, it was hard to see how the New Year could be anything other than good.

Jim introduced Tom to his boss, J. Aldrich Parker, a large powerfully built man with an entirely bald head, his eyes bouncing around the room as he talked then quickly flicking back to Tom. Parker, totally self absorbed and pre-occupied, interested and disinterested all at the same time, addressed himself to Tom,

"So tell me, Tom, why don't we have you working for us?"
He didn't wait for a reply, but continued on,
"You must have some of your brother's talents, and that's something we can always use in this organization. Yes Sir,

Jim is part of what it takes to make it all work and boy, are we going to make it work this coming year. You know Jim was a key factor in our purchase of the Midon Corporation, now that is going to change the whole damn game! We are going to show this goddam world just what the US can do in business. We are goin' to kick some ass. And then we have the new biotech business, that's going to be really big and we are going to be a major player, yes sir! So tell me what is your line, Tom?"

"I'm concerned with finance mainly these days."

"Damn right, finance is what it's all about. The bottom line ain't right, nothin' else matters a damn, Jim knows all about that, I can tell you, don't you Jim? Sales targets and keeping the cost of production right down, that's what it's all about. Now with this new situation in Ireland, peace and all, maybe we should look at a new European production plant there, what do you say Jim?

Again Parker didn't wait for a reply, but his voice changed down a gear, still urgent but now becoming darker and more sombre in tone,
"But you'll have to excuse us now Tom, right now Jim and I need go talk with our Japanese distributor, our old friend Hiroshi over there. I told the waiters to pour a quantity of liquor into him so he's loosened up some. Jim and I need go find out just what the hell's happening in his patch, see

if he's up to handling the new product line, that right Jim? Tom, it's been real good talking with you."

He stretched out his right hand and solidly shook Tom's hand, almost simultaneously placing his left hand on Jim's arm and leading him off through the crowd in the direction of a small Japanese man who was busy smiling and nodding to what looked like another of the Parker-Wotton executives.

*       *       *

It wasn't until Saturday, January 1 that Tom and Jim first talked about what brought Tom to California. In the afternoon they went into his "den" as he called the book lined office he had for his own use at home. State of the art computer, fax machine, three phones, beautiful modern furnishings, soft chairs with a view over the ocean. Walls decorated with abstracts and sailing pictures. His sailing trophies arranged on a shelf. They sat down with their drinks while Art Pepper was blowing alto sax from the stereo system, light, bright and full of life.

Jim with his elegant casual clothes, slight American accent, suggesting success and power, assurance, everything was possible. Gone was the apparent disillusionment Jim had expressed in their conversation on the night of Christmas Eve, Jim Ryan had the assurance and all the trappings of an extremely successful man,

"It was really nice having you here for the Holiday's Tom, we don't see enough of each other. Time goes by, everyone is so damn busy. The rate we're going we'll all be dead soon!"

For Tom, this was an all too appropriate opening to what was sure to be a difficult conversation,
"Yes indeed, that's true."

Politics as they related to Northern Ireland was not something they normally discussed in any detail. They didn't see the Irish problem in the same terms, it had brought enough trouble into the family for one lifetime. Jim regarded it as tribal, primitive, couldn't understand how the Irish could get on so well once out of Ireland and still fail to sort themselves out in that tiny under-populated country. The unresolved problem made no sense as part of the modern world. The barbarities of the IRA and their mirror image, the various Protestant Terrorist groups, were obscenities, an affront to civilized living. He would have nothing to do with any US/ Ireland organization, and for sure, no contributions to Noraid were ever going to come from him. He wanted to stay well separated from it all.

"Anyway Tom, how are things with you?"

"Well, that's what I need to talk to you about. Knowing your views as I do, this is more than a little difficult for me.

You know I got involved again with the IRA after '69. Really these days I am just processing funds for them — yes I know what you think about it all, all the violence, but let's try to leave that for the moment. My problem is they now want to kill me."

It wasn't usual for Jim Ryan to show strong emotions, but this time he did,

"Jesus H. Christ, Tom! You know my opinion, you should never had gotten involved again. I know how it looked in '69, but that place is a festering cesspit. It will never be right. And the atrocities that have been committed cannot be justified for anything. It will just corrupt the entire country and everyone who gets involved. It's sickening. No one outside the place can understand it. Since we can't wait for the entire planet to self-destruct and solve the problem, as an immediate solution the whole damn population of Northern Ireland should be given one way tickets to well separated locations and the place cleared out. Either plant it with forest or invite the Hong Kong Chinese to come in."

Nothing was said for a few minutes, the effect Tom's announcement had was all too obvious. Behind Jim's outburst of anger, Tom knew that Jim was already sensing the impact of the problem on all their lives, it's seriousness and it's immediate ability to affect his own life and that of his family. Jim spoke again, still angry,

"I don't want this stuff brought into my home, I don't want Ellen and the kids in danger. I don't want any part of it!"

Tom waited for a few moments before he responded, knowing that Jim would eventually calm down and apply his mind to the problem,
"I know that. I don't believe there is any immediate danger. But the IRA is not like a golf club, you can't just tell them you are not renewing your subscription."

"What the hell do they want to kill you for anyway, I thought you were one of their goddam heroes?"

"That was all a long time ago, things have changed. The whole organization is totally different, different people, different methods."

"Yes a damn sight nastier from what everyone can see. They now have no limits at all on the depths to which they will go."

"The problem is fighting a modern State which is prepared to use underhand methods and which has all the resources of the State. It ends up the same way anywhere in the world. These are the only tactics available, the only ones that are sustainable in the long term. From a general philosophical point of view, I might argue that all States are finally controlled by violence of one sort or another. Police forces and armies. If you step out of line, we'll put you in jail, have your freedom taken away at least. Freedom and democracy are limited notions as they are actually practised. You can't opt out and declare yourself a democracy of one person or get together as a small group outside the existing State, declare yourself independent of the State, like some militant groups are trying to do in the US. But the hell with all that, I've had enough of the arguments, enough of the violence, I want to get out now. If I can live long enough to get out."

He told of the robbery, how it had gone wrong and the position he was now in,
"I don't know if I'm being framed, set up or what. The fact that everyone directly involved is dead is incredible. No simple robbery like that has ever gone so wrong. It could have been blown by an informer, or by one of the Intelligence Services or it could be some kind of internal plot. But my head is next on the block. I've been left with the responsibility for cash that's not there, on the back of an operation that went completely wrong. The only prospect of survival I have is that if I can get the money back, then I am sure I can get out of the IRA, no matter what the background story is to all this."

In fact he wasn't at all so sure, but the situation seemed to require some positive input of optimism about the future from him. Jim spoke again, a little calmer now,

"Well the first thing is that you can hardly stay here for much longer. Let's hope the bastards haven't been tracking you too carefully."

"No, they should be checking alcohol treatment centres first. But they will come after me. I'm sure of that."

"Why alcohol treatment centres?"

"That's where I told the Regional Development Authority I was going when I left."

A grimace of a smile passed across Jim's face as he replied, "With the number of well populated centres around Ireland, that should keep them busy for a little while. But maybe the alcohol centre is not a bad idea."

"How do you mean?"

"Well you certainly can't stay in hotels. Credit cards are a great convenience, they're also an ideal way to track someone."

"Yes, I know that."

Jim, leaning forward slightly, continued,
"Believe it or not, I know a priest here, who runs an enormous centre for all sorts of odd modern ills. Don't worry, I haven't found religion, I had enough of that in Ireland. I

got to know him when we had a problem with one of the Corporate Vice Presidents. No, this guy is civilized, perhaps a little odd by my standards, but he runs a very big centre in the desert where he treats all sorts of misfits. Alcoholics, heroin addicts, child molesters, perverts, whatever. All that's needed is lots of money. It's very big business, plush and expensive, but your friends would have a job finding you there. Not the sort of place for your average Irish navvy after a few too many."

"Sounds OK. Should help me stay alive for a little while longer. The remaining problem is how to get the funds to repay the IRA?"

"One problem at a time. How much do you need?"

"About $400,000 that probably means more like $500,000 to cover everything involved."

"I don't have that kind of money easily available. I'll have to think about it, there must be a solution. Just promise me, if you get out of this, no more, this is the last IRA problem I ever want to see. I'm doing this not just for you, but for the old folks. I don't want them going into their grave on the basis of this shit and you dead."

The twinge of guilt Jim felt about his old affair with Hazel, he left that out. There were enough problems already in the family without that. But he wondered if he had helped de-stabilize Tom's marriage. Jesus, Tom wasn't the only one who had generated problems in his youth. But there was little that could be done about all that now, except maybe help find a way out of this mess.

# Chapter 11

The Christmas/New Year period had been one of intense frustration for O'Sullivan. Everything was closed down, even revolutionaries took a holiday break with their families. Tom Ryan was gone and he couldn't do anything further to track him. The situation with Belfast was getting worse as he tried to explain that not only had the robbery gone disastrously wrong, that the proceeds were missing, now he had to tell them Ryan was missing and he couldn't find him. His conversation with Hazel Ryan had not been useful. He had called the Western Regional Development Authority before Christmas, but got nowhere, he tried again when their offices re-opened after the holidays on Tuesday, January 4,

"Could you put me through to Tom Ryan, darlin'?"

That creep again with the Northern accent,

"Mr. Ryan is out of the office, can anyone else help you?"

"No, I need to speak to Tom Ryan urgently, how can I reach him?"

"Mr. Ryan is on leave."

"I see. When will he be back from leave?"

"I can't say, would you like to speak with someone else?"

"No I fucking wouldn't."

He swore again after putting the phone down, damn stupid bitch, how many times did she have to be told what he wanted. The following day he tried again, this time speaking to Duggan and saying he was a personal friend who needed to contact Tom urgently. Duggan just said he was away on indefinite leave.

"But you are expecting him back?"

"Yes, of course, probably in about six weeks to two months time."

"Do you know where he is, I need to contact him very urgently?"

"No, I don't know where he is."

O'Sullivan put the phone down again and swore. He was sure the bastard knew. All very odd. The fact that Duggan said he was expecting him back meant nothing of course. There was nothing for it, he would have to phone Belfast again. He reported to his contact, as usual using one of the pre-assigned call box numbers. He was told he would get a call back next evening, at 8pm. He was surprised to find a woman calling him,

"I hear you have a problem?"

"Yes, Tom Ryan is missing and I can't find him. He's gone from his apartment, I've contacted his ex-wife and the people he works with, no one knows where he is or at least won't say. I'm sure he's done a runner with the proceeds of the robbery and I want him found."

"No doubt you do. If what you say is true, we'll all be very anxious to find him indeed."

The sarcasm in her voice wasn't lost on him, but he continued, business-like,
"There can be no doubt about it. Can you track him down?"

"You want me to track him down? I'm not allocating my scarce and valuable resources to that."

"Why not, surely it's important enough?"

"Oh it's important alright, but I'm not risking our personnel in something that you should be able to handle."

"Me?"

"Yes, you. What would you do if you had a relative missing and didn't want to contact the police? Think about it. Use your wits if you have any and make sure you keep us out of it."

She put the phone down and he stood there, listening to dial tone. O'Sullivan was left feeling small and ridiculous, like when he was a little boy again, stirring up old corners of his mind, making him feel inadequate again.

No one had ever liked O'Sullivan. Not when he was a kid, not since. In a world where the generality of human kind muddle through, make compromises, accept the little hurts and rejections handed to them, the beautiful and those with inherited wealth gain lifelong, life enhancing advantages that no amount of effort or even intelligence can ever compensate for. In the case of the naturally beautiful, the world seems to smile on them from the beginning, defining a good world for them to live in, where everything is always that much easier. So their beauty is reflected back to them and enhanced and it seems they stride through life in a different way from the rest of us. Those with inherited wealth take the world on from a position of security and style which the world happily reinforces for them. O'Sullivan was certainly not beautiful but then, he was not particularly ugly. He had no inherited wealth, but neither did he know anything that could be described as disabling poverty. The post-war caring social structure of the British State had made sure of that for him and the rest of those living in Northern Ireland. It was just in that other great divide in humankind that he had faired so badly. He was unfortunately cast among those who regarded life as naturally miserable, those who could only be satisfied when all those around them were reduced to a similar state of misery. As he grew older, this trait only got worse in him. Perhaps it was genetic, perhaps environmental, but he became more like his mother, worrying about everything, unable to relax, there was no pleasure to be found in life. So now it seemed there was just something fundamentally unattractive about him, it seemed like no one had ever loved him and the world had never smiled kindly on him. Always slightly overweight, ever since he was a kid. There was nothing in this world that of itself ever made him happy, he had never loved anyone. He was no good at sports. At school he had been bullied, laughed at, pushed around and made feel small and unimportant by the other kids. No good at any type of social interaction. Didn't drink so he didn't go to pubs. Didn't have anything interesting to say. But all that had changed when he was courted by the IRA group in University. They had assured him he was an important part of the struggle and welcomed him.

He put the phone down and consoled himself, tried to re-build his confidence in his objectives. He knew he had done his best, he was sure of that. The problems of the failed robbery and Ryan's disappearance were not of his making, but these things had occupied him totally in the period between Christmas and New Year. When he found couldn't contact Ryan by phone, O'Sullivan had gone around to check Tom Ryan's apartment. No one in. No sign of the car. Next day he had tried again. Same thing. O'Sullivan then decided it was time to try the family. The ex-wife seemed like a good possibility. From what he heard, she didn't feel she need do Ryan any favours. Not since the marriage break up two years ago. It was the first day of the New Year, Saturday afternoon, before he found her at home and her neighbours had already started looking at him suspiciously because he had visited the empty cottage so often. But Hazel Ryan hadn't been useful to him. In fact he had been surprised to find he received a distinctly frosty reception. Her cottage looked almost as desolate as his own home, except hers was much cleaner, but he didn't notice that. She had put up a few Christmas decorations, but it didn't look too festive. Nor too homely.

Maybe she knew something and was on guard against questions? No, he rejected that possibility, she really didn't seem to know what had happened to Ryan. Said she had no contact with him these days. He could be anywhere for all she knew. Or cared by the sounds of her. But then she had said Ryan might be with his brother in California and then she looked like she regretted saying it. Well, it was at least a possibility, he hadn't known Ryan had a brother and the way she had let it slip looked real enough for this to be a possible lead.

O'Sullivan had never liked Ryan, regarding Ryan as one of

the old timers, something left over from the distant, ineffectual past, all romantic rubbish with no results. All that business about having been active on the Border in the Fifties, that cut no ice with O'Sullivan. Or being in Derry in '69. Fucking Hero, but Ryan was too old now, didn't have the drive for the modern struggle. Didn't understand modern urban terrorism didn't see where the Movement was going. Hadn't the guts for it. How it had to be unrelenting, total war.

Then he started to think how best to turn the situation to his own advantage. It was men like him that the IRA needed, those who could plan ruthlessly and would push the armed struggle forward so that they could force the British to yield. He wasn't fazed by the shock of each bombing, it was necessary. Loss of life was necessary, civilian casualties were necessary. The more stark the violence, the better. The more shock the better, the more the British tabloids went into hysterics the better. The lessons of history were clear, the British had done the same thing in Cyprus, Aden, Kenya and all the other ex-colonies before they pulled out. The same old headlines, "Our poor honourable British Tommies being shot in the back by terrorists". They would never learn. Violence was the only way, this was the lesson of history.

His reflections and analysis restored his confidence after

the humiliation he felt from the phone call. Given time and resources, he had no doubt he would track Ryan down and take him out. It was always necessary that clear decisive action be taken to enforce discipline and he had hoped the IRA would have taken immediate action or at least arranged for "Trial in Abstentia", followed by execution as soon as they found him. Now he was left to handle the whole problem by himself, he would show them, show them what he was made of. He was the one who had organized so many successful street protests in the North, before they sent him down South. That damn bitch on the phone would eat her words, next time he would be shown respect, he deserved nothing less. He started with the Dublin edition of the classified pages, first looking under "detectives" and then cross checking under "security".

*          *          *

On Tuesday, January 10, fifteen minutes late for his 11.00am appointment, O'Sullivan pressed the bell beside the brass plate saying "John Seymour & Associates, Security Services" one of a group of business name plates beside the Georgian entrance door at the top of the short run of granite steps. The address he had come to was in Lower Leeson Street, in Dublin's nightlife district. The basement he noted contained a nightclub called "Strippers". In the aftermath of peace, when they were in a position to exercise power, he would close such places down.

The intercom voiced a pleasant female response that irritated him,

"Yes, can I help you?"

"Blake, I have an appointment with John Seymour for eleven."

"Please come in Mr. Blake."

The buzzer sounded and he pushed the door open and entered the large, high entrance hall which had had it's intricate plasterwork decorations picked out and highlighted in different coloured paints. The receptionist looked out at him through a sliding glass panel in the wall,

"If you go up to the fourth floor Mr. Blake, Mr. Seymour is expecting you."

After the second floor, the quality and the width of the stairway diminished. By the time he reached the fourth floor he was out of breath and knew his progress was being monitored by the series of video cameras at each stairway landing. The decor had moved from any claim to the original Georgian and was now plain and simple modern and all done in white paint. The fourth floor landing was occupied by a young guy with close cropped black hair sitting at a computer terminal, with three other small video screens beside him. The young guy looked intelligent and

fit, like a muscular accountant, O'Sullivan thought, as he
was addressed by Madden,

"Good morning Mr. Blake, please knock and go straight
in, Mr. Seymour is expecting you."

The voice was no nonsense, clear and full of confidence,
courteous but very definite about what was expected.
O'Sullivan didn't like the look or the authoritative sound
of him, it was as if he was ordering O'Sullivan about. He
just opened the door and walked into the room, which was
obviously formed in the attic from what would have been
the servant's quarters in the original house. The room was
painted white with a modern business desk and the back-
side of a computer facing towards him. The room seemed
remote from the world, disconnected, floating god-like
above the affairs of the mortals below. At the far side of
the desk stood a slightly built man, black well cut suit, white
shirt and red tie, light brown hair going slightly grey, pale
face, but the most noticeable thing about him was the pale
piercing blue eyes which seemed to bore through O'Sullivan while reaching out a hand in greeting,

"Please sit down and tell me what I can do for you, Mr.
Blake. By the way, how did you select us?"

"Oh, I found you in the classified phone directory, the
golden pages as you call them down here, listed under

security. Your advert said you did personal and business security, provided bodyguards for celebrities and had international facilities."

"I see, so what can I do for you?"

While absentmindedly straightening the objects on his desk, Seymour pressed a tiny switch on the side of the desk telephone system and initiated a camera sequence that took several exposures of O'Sullivan through a pinhole in the wall behind Seymour. They already had him on videotape, but the still shots were generally the most useful and convenient.

"I need to find someone who has disappeared. He is a friend and business partner of mine and it's possible he has gone to the States to his brother in California. He may have mistakenly taken a lot of money with him, so the matter is delicate. I need you to locate him for me so that I can make contact. I presume your international associates could do that?"

"Yes I'm sure we can get an investigation under way. Do you have a photograph of Mr. Ryan?"

"No actually I don't, he was one of those people who don't like having their photograph taken. You probably know the type."

· "Yes, I've known a few who felt like that. So when did all this happen and how did you get to know about his disappearance."

Seymour listened impassively to the tale he was told, most people who came into his office told him lies. With women, clients or otherwise, this was always the case in Seymour's experience, even when they didn't have any demanding reason for lying, they lied, as though they needed to create their own private version of reality. Like a priest, you slowly sickened hearing the sins, small and large, of the world unburdening itself. You listen, understand, are sympathetic, grant them forgiveness, tell them it will now be alright, but unlike the priest, Seymour was expected to actually put the world right for them. To go out and seek their justice, rob and spy for them, take revenge for them. As a kind of antidote to this murky world he was continually invited into, he dressed immaculately in his office, to establish and maintain a feeling of cleanliness, order, wellbeing, separation.

But the danger bells were starting to ring now for Seymour, the Northern Ireland accent, the lack of human warmth or even the normality's of human weakness, no feeling of empathy, all this he saw before him and it bothered him. The Mid-West town Blake gave as his address, it was too damn near where Maguire had staged the disastrous robbery that cost him his life. After Maguire's death, Seymour had been sure that was an end to his own fringe involvement with the schemes of the IRA. He looked at Blake, this guy had the feel of death about him.

Since leaving London and going "legit" with his security business, Seymour was always walking a knife-edge between criminality and the law, spending his life in the murky underbelly of modern society, it's lies and deceits. He always needed to be on guard, this Blake didn't feel right to him. He didn't like this character, not that he liked most of his customers, but at least he could usually figure their motives. He weighed up the unattractive figure opposite him, a fidgety man, trying to be cleverer than he is, thinking his deviousness would not be found out,

"OK, based on what you tell us, our American associates should be able to help. It will cost, of course, their retainer, say five thousand dollars, plus ours, plus expenses, say six thousand pounds altogether as your first payment to us before we start."

Seymour had pitched it high, it was one further way to check out the seriousness of the game he was being invited into. O'Sullivan opened the zippered brown document case he had with him and counted off six thousand pounds in large denomination notes,
"I presume that should get you started then."

"Certainly, Mr. Blake. I'll be in touch with you as soon as I have anything to report, but it may take some time from the limited information you have given us before we have anything, we are starting cold and California is a big place."

When O'Sullivan left, Seymour sat down and considered what to do. The name Blake he could easily check against the unlisted private number Blake had given him, a single phone call would get him the name. Many of his clients didn't fully realize that in the two-way nature of the process of getting the information they asked for, he almost invariably found out about their own dark murky secrets as part of the web in which they had involved themselves. The answer came back, the phone number Blake had given him was listed under O'Sullivan. Not that it was unusual for people to use false names, but this thing was developing a very dangerous feel to it.

Maybe drugs, the availability of a large cash down-payment was in keeping with that, but maybe it was even worse. Terrorism would be more unusual, but this O'Sullivan didn't fit into any other probable category. As Sherlock Holmes used to say, when you have eliminated all but one possibility, what you are left with is the inevitable, no matter how unlikely. Damn it, if Maguire was still alive, he would be the obvious one to check this out with. Who else was there to turn to with this kind of shit, he needed to be very careful.

He went into the small room off his office where he had a wardrobe packed with a strange variety of clothes useful to him in the course of his work. In the room there was also a wash hand basin and a toilet. He closed the lid of the toilet and stood on top to reach up to the oversized, painted metal wall plate covering the extractor fan and pulled it off it's fixings using both his hands. Beside the fan there was a small fireproof safe mounted in the wall. The six thousand pounds cash he put into the safe and withdrew one of the computer discs that contained his personal files, files comprising the most secret information he had gathered over the years. He replaced the covering panel and went back into the office and loaded the disc into the computer. He was sure he remembered the ever-careful Maguire giving him another name, for a rainy day, just in case. Eventually he found it, listed in a file he had called "emergencies" and there he also saw the name of Tom Ryan. Now he had no doubt about what he was getting into. He dialled the Galway number,

"Could I speak to Mr. McIntyre?"

"He's not here."

"If I give you my name and number maybe you could ask him to call me?"

She didn't sound to keen, but he gave her the name and

number. Then the inevitable check, blunt and to the point in her flat country monotone, but seemingly disinterested, "And what is it you want?"

"It's a personal matter, tell him I knew the late Danny Maguire in London many years ago and he told me to contact Mr. McIntyre sometime."

She said nothing, just hung up.

*       *       *

It was several days later before McIntyre got back to Galway in his old trawler, but he already knew Seymour was looking for him and that somehow it had to be connected to IRA business and he should move very carefully, as always.

# Chapter 12

It would be a bitterly cold ride to Galway. But Seymour wanted to experience the freedom of the bike and the weather was about as good as he could hope for in January. Seymour had dressed as warmly as possible, but he also wanted to feel the inevitable stimulating bite of the cold, use the pain to stay hard as the cold worked it's way through the all in one outer suit and the underlying warm protective layers. The electrically controlled gate closed automatically behind him as he rode out of his detached house in the southern suburbs of Dublin, leaving the myriad electronic security devices to look after his property. The twin cylinder engine of the red BMW R1100 RS revved eagerly and he reached forward and switched on the handle bar warmers, checked the ABS failure warning lights had gone out. On the winter roads, this added measure of safety he regarded as a necessary feature. He tucked himself into the bikes slim sports fairing and accelerated away in the pre-dawn darkness of the winter morning beating the morning traffic to the roads. He stopped off at Kinnegad as the sun started to lighten the sky and had breakfast, then continued for the next sixty minutes as the powerful motorcycle consumed the ribbon of road until he reached the city of Galway, winding his way through and out again on the coast road north of the city. Now seeing the landscape take on its unique rock strewn, barren and wind-blown, desolate character until he reached the small harbour where McIntyre lived and kept his trawler.

The house adjoined a small pub that displayed a large colourfully painted, wall-mounted menu offering a wide variety of fresh fish dishes. The sun was shinning brightly now on this crisp, clear winters morning and it was possible to imagine how the pretty setting would attract the tourists in the summer. He parked the bike around the back of the pub carpark, out of sight, getting off stiffly, the cold deep in his bones.

It seemed McIntyre's wife must run the pub and that it was her he spoke with in his first telephone call, for McIntyre led him directly through from the house into the deserted interior of the pub. The pub was small with a low ceiling, dark and asleep this early in the morning, strangely silent and still, church like. The air cool, dank with the sweet smell of stale beer and the lingering remnants of the cutting sharpness of years of cigarette smoke. McIntyre, small, squat and strong, his black straight hair sticking out in shocks from his head, face unshaven, he exuded a suppressed energy, his dark brown eyes scanning Seymour's face, checking and re-checking. Seymour declined the offer of a drink, instead asking for coffee. McIntyre switched on the machine and came back and seated himself on a wooden kitchen type chair on the far side of the round dark wooden table, stained with beer marks. McIntyre had poured himself a large whiskey,

"So, tell me Mr. Seymour, just how does someone like you know Danny Maguire?"

"I worked with him in London in the Sixties. We were mates and looked after each other. It all got a little hot for us after a while and we had to leave in a hurry. We went our own separate ways then back here. I started my detective agency, providing Minders for personalities and so on. But I owed Maguire and he used me occasionally to help out with his projects. This was on a commercial and purely personal basis, I have no connection or interest in the organization and don't want any. But because of our unusual relationship and the fact that he knew I could have problems if anything happened to him, he gave me your name as the one to go to. So I'm here."

"And you have a problem, I suppose, but first I want some more detailed assurance that you are what you say."

"Yes, I have a problem, and if I tell you I was involved in disabling a security guard as a side event in Maguire's last operation, does that reassure you?"

"Maybe so, first tell me about London and why you felt indebted to Maguire."

"That was all a long time ago, I don't talk about it."

McIntyre sat back in his chair and waved a powerful open hand in a sweeping, encompassing gesture,
"Mr. Seymour, have you any idea of the dangerous place you have entered, you are in the Lion's Den so to speak, I can assure you this is not the occasion to be reticent."

"Well, I was in another Lion's Den in London. A club owner thought I was having it away with his pretty young wife. I was down on the club floor late one night with a shotgun to my head thinking this was my last, when Maguire walked in. He was a sight for sore eyes, and for the sore rest of me. I can see him still, the big bulk of him moving smooth and easy, grinning all over his face, like he was walking into a party. The guy with the shotgun swung it up and away from my head to blast Maguire, but he wasn't quick enough. Maguire took him out and then took out the club owner."

"Sounds like rough times right enough. That put an end to your fooling with the wife."

"Except I wasn't fooling around with her at all. She fed my name to her husband to protect her real lover. So I nearly got finished off. She, of course, became a rich young widow, which suited her very well."

There was a pause while McIntyre enjoyed his whiskey,
"Yeah, that's more or less what I heard about the pair of

you leaving London. Not that Maguire said much about the details of that or of what you did for him later, when the two of you were back in this green and pleasant land, but your story fits. So, Mr. Seymour, what do you want?"

"About a week ago I had a visit from a guy calling himself Blake, but whose real name is O'Sullivan from Castleglen. He wants me to find a man called Tom Ryan for him. I'm not sure what this is all about. This is a photograph of O'Sullivan and this is one I tracked down for Tom Ryan. Can you help me?"

McIntyre got up from his chair and looked down at Seymour,
"I'll make your coffee, sit where you are. How do you like it?"

"Strong, black and with sugar."

McIntyre went behind the bar,
"It would probably save me a lot of trouble if I shot you now, save you a lot of trouble too."

McIntyre turned round unsmiling but holding a cup of coffee and a sugar bowl,
"You are in deep water Mr. Seymour."

He paused, still on the far side of the bar, picked up the whiskey bottle, balancing the precarious cup and saucer on

the sugar bowl in his right hand and then came forward
round the bar again,

"And you are a cool customer walking in here with this
stuff. Have you any idea of the risk you've taken?"

"I seem to have got used to risk as a part of life. Can you
help?"

McIntyre sat himself down again,

"Risk is hardly the word for it. Unlike so many in this little
country of ours, Danny Maguire never suffered from verbal
diarrhoea. I liked that and I liked him. He always delivered
more than he promised, God rest him. If he gave you my
name then it matters to me. Let me tell you how it is."

McIntyre took another sip of whiskey and continued,

"Maguire and myself were in the IRA since we were
youngsters. And so was Tom Ryan, though he came from
Dublin and I didn't know him all that well. We were all up
in Dublin for weekend training, running around the bloody
Wicklow Mountains with a mad bastard who had deserted
from the British Army giving us what he called military
training. You could hardly understand him between his
being alcoholic and having a half-English, half-Irish accent.
The armaments we had were damn near useless and the
training not much better, but we all thought we were all
going to be feckin' heroes and run the British Army out of
Ireland. The only one who made it to hero was Tom Ryan.

The poor bastard was sent up North in the pouring rain one winters night, dropped off a truck this side of the border with two others and told to attack a check-point. Fucking madness. The other two were shot dead and Ryan nearly got the left side of his face shot off. You could say he was lucky, but the bastards gave him a rough time when they found him of course, nearly kicked him to death in the field where he was captured. So he was one of the few of us who ended up in jail for his trouble. But like the rest of us he'd had enough of the pointlessness of it all in the Fifties, so when he got out of jail he stayed away. That was until sixty-nine and the renewed fun and games in the North. Since then it's all been more serious, right up to the present cease-fire. Who knows, maybe it will all be sorted out? It's hard to believe we've got this far, but not everyone in the organization thinks this will work out. The signs aren't good. So that's Ryan and Maguire. O'Sullivan is different. I don't like him. He's young, from the North and ambitious. He's an office boy, but a very dangerous office boy since he has no idea of what it takes out there, not like the late Danny Maguire. From what I hear, O'Sullivan was getting beyond himself in organizing street protests in the middle of the cease-fire and generally making a nuisance of himself, so they sent him down here."

"Do you think I'm being set up somehow, by O'Sullivan?"

"From what you've told me, he shouldn't even know you exist, Maguire would never have told him."

"But he does know I exist, he's come to me asking me to find Tom Ryan. Why does he want Ryan?"

McIntyre grunted and looked down at his whiskey,
"What I've heard is that the funds from the robbery in Castleglen are missing. Maybe he thinks Ryan has taken the proceeds. That's bloody ridiculous as anyone who knows Ryan will tell you, but then", he shrugged and opened his hands in a gesture of despair, "I suppose you don't have to find him, you could just stay in and see what happens, how could that cause you problems?"

"If the IRA think I'm taking a fee and playing games with them, it could cause me problems, the kind of problems I don't want."

"You probably have no alternative right now, you have to stay in to find out what it's all about and why you've been involved."

McIntyre stood up, saying
"Just be careful and remember this conversation never took place and I never met you."

As Seymour pulled down the dark visor on the helmet and rode out of the carpark, he was aware that a visiting stranger would be noticed by just about everyone in the little fishing hamlet. His visit was hardly a secret. But he could be sure, no one would talk. And no doubt, he thought, if McIntyre hadn't been satisfied, he would now be taking a one way sea voyage in the hold of a trawler.

# Chapter 13

It was 10.00am, Saturday January 21, 1995 as Jim Ryan swung his silver 500 SL Mercedes sports convertible through the entrance to Mount Abraham and parked near reception. He wondered again if that wily old Jesuit had chosen the name to ensure that his Jewish clients felt comfortable. Probably, always an eye for business, despite the Patrician aura of spirituality he gave off. The Catholic Church merged with American Business Methods. A great combination.

A sweeping expanse of interconnected white buildings faced him, while behind him water sprinklers played on lawns spreading between flowering bushes and tall trees. Mexican gardeners tending the grounds, keeping everything in a state of perfection. California Spanish was perhaps the way to describe the impression it made. It looked like a large and expensive country club. America at it's best. The receptionist was quite beautiful, classic California. Tall with high cheekbones, long blond hair tied back. He couldn't see the long legs, but he was sure they were there. An instant cure for the perverted clientele he thought, straight sex with her would be OK anytime.

Tom and Jim walked through the grounds, it was warm and

sunny, an idyllic day in this beautiful peaceful environment. Jim started to talk about the problem of how to find the money for the IRA,

"On paper Tom I'm financially OK. Even paying for the kids at College, the Medical Insurance, Pension Plan and so on. The Parker-Wotton Corporation has been good for me, I own a lot of stock options and some stock, but I can't sell without giving them notice. In fact to sell it off at all in the present phase of the business cycle would be bad news. In any event, it would leave the family exposed. The kind of job I do in Marketing is high risk, the business is not what it used to be in the days of the cold war where the government was issuing big orders for the military work. We're all scared shitless about the way the instrument business is going, the whole marketplace is being kicked to bits with overcapacity and prices going through the floor. I can't expose the family to the possible risk of taking half a million dollars out of our security by any method. On the other hand, we are all sitting targets right now, including my family who have nothing to do with this."

"So what can we do?"

"Crazy as it may sound, the idea I have is to rob something. Something which I can get and which I know is saleable for really big money. But you have to get involved with a piece of this plan."

"It's my problem, naturally I'll do whatever is necessary! But how can someone in your position get involved in a robbery, think of the risks to you?"

"This is how I see it. The Japanese instrument manufacturers are becoming a real pain in the neck. Despite all the US Government action, the Japanese home market is effectively closed to us. Half of the little we ship in, they take to bits and use it to get technical and manufacturing information. They have a locked up home market that they use to develop their own product lines at high prices. Then they release selected models into the US and world markets at rock bottom prices. They want to take a piece of this business, a big piece, just like they did with the car business. That's their plan. So far they have been contained. But they want every possible way forward. I intend to give them a little help for the price of your life."

"Go on."

"I can get them a piece of technology they want, an X-ray detector. It's tiny, like a computer chip. It's also new and has all sorts of advances in it. It threatens to take them out of one whole segment in the instrument business. An entire instrument line of theirs will be as obsolete as the model T Ford and they know that. We need to set up a contact with the Japanese, one that keeps me as clear of the whole process as possible. I'll give you all the information, you have to set it up, I will deliver the goods."

"But what happens then, even if it all works according to plan, what happens to your career? You'll be destroyed."

"I reckon I can look after myself, always have. Just make sure you do exactly as I say, this is my plan, it has to go my way. There have been some strange telephone calls to the house, including some hang up calls. It may be that your former friends are already trying to track you through me, maybe even trying to set-up a break-in at the house to check it for signs of you. We don't have much choice and we don't have much time."

"Yes, I know that. I'm getting more paranoid by the day here."

"You'll have to make the contact through Kara, it's the only way the Japanese will deal with us. I know them too well through my contacts with the Parker-Wotton agents in Japan. There is no way they would trust us as Westerners going directly to them."

# Chapter 14

When Seymour returned from visiting McIntyre in Galway, he contacted an acquaintance who worked for the FBI in California and called in a favour. He asked him to see if there was any trace of a Tom Ryan entering the USA from Ireland. The reply had come back that Ryan had entered at New York Kennedy on Monday, December 19 last, with an address of the Sheraton Center Hotel and that he had checked out the following day. He had made no phone calls from the hotel. That was all that was immediately available. Seymour asked him to keep the file active and report back if anything new showed up. He then asked a private detective agency to check if Tom Ryan was at his brother's house. But first they had to identify his brother and that would take some time. Two weeks later the answer came back, they had checked and he was not staying at his brother's house. Then the FBI contact came back to him to say that Tom Ryan had left the USA on a flight for Frankfurt.

Seymour put in a call to O'Sullivan and told him Ryan was in the States but was not staying with his brother. Investigations were continuing. O'Sullivan was not happy at the lack of progress.

"I'm calling in favours here, Mr. Blake, and that costs money. Do you want me to continue?"

O'Sullivan didn't like the thoughts of more money going out, but then he remembered the woman he was reporting to in Belfast, and reluctantly he again committed himself to the course of action he had started,

"Right, I'll drop an envelope through your main office door this weekend, cash. Just make sure you find Ryan."

*     *     *

For Tom Ryan there had been no question of going into Dublin, or London, Frankfurt was the best choice available. He was no longer sure what was happening back in Ireland. The IRA or the Security Services could be tracking him, Dublin was far too dangerous. By now he could have been fingered to the British or the British might have started to take an interest in him again with the odd goings on around Castleglen. Once a terrorist always a terrorist on their files. London was out. Even Frankfurt wasn't without risk. From Frankfurt, he took a train to Dusseldorf. Kara flew directly from Dublin to Dusseldorf.

She was waiting for him at the train station, softly smiling as always. Her brown eyes taking in every detail of him. Knowing him by just looking at him. He was tanned with the sunshine of California in winter. They took a taxi the short distance to the Steigenberger Hotel. This was a brief opportunity to be together, they might as well have some luxury. To help maintain security, Kara made the reservation in her name and on her credit card. In any event, his cash situation was not good, he was relying on Jim for funds. Even though his salary was being paid into his bank account, he couldn't touch it. In the taxi he reached over to her,

"I've missed you so much. There's been so much time alone to think."

"So what did you think about?" she asked smiling brightly at him and anticipating his reply.

He put his hand up her long skirt. She was already wet with desire.

"Probably the same things you think about!" and kissed her passionately and long.

"I do love you Ry-san."

"That's good!"

The lightness of his reply covered the fact that he knew what they had to discuss now was going to bring them into the one area of conflict in their love for each other. They emerged from the taxi at the imposing hotel entrance, the parking area full of Ferrari's and other similarly exotic forms of transport. When they checked in, he asked for coffee to be brought to their room.

As they sipped the coffee, he explained the whole situation again to her. How he was trapped, it was only a matter of time before the IRA got to him. What he had to do to get out. How Jim was to help. They needed her to find a Japanese contact, someone who would set up the deal, take care of handling the merchandise.

He knew who she would go to, Bansan. She had told him about Bansan, meeting him on the flight to Paris. She claimed she didn't love Bansan, described their continuing relationship as intellectual, business, friendship. A Japanese compartmentalization of life. She didn't love Bansan, not the way she loved Tom. But she wouldn't put him out of her life either. For Tom Ryan this was crazy, he couldn't accept it, wanted them to have each other without anyone else. Total, committed romantic love. Now he knew he was asking her to go to Bansan. It was the only way the deal could be set up. No Japanese would enter such an arrangement directly with a Westerner. It required the Japanese trust of each other, it required favours to be done, between those who had known each other for a long time. Where there was complete trust. Bansan had helped with the finance to get her language school started in Dublin. There was a long-standing bond between them.

When they went to bed it was not the usual simple, happy, easy relationship they enjoyed. They had been apart for weeks and both were filled with desire, he wanted her in the simple loving way they had been blessed with. But a spectre had been brought directly into their lives and stood between them. Tom Ryan was using the very relationship he objected to, that between Kara and Bansan, for his own ends. She too was unhappy. Two worlds she had kept apart were meeting. She was caught in this complex web of relationships. Caught by her love of this big Irishman. Caught by honour and commitment to Bansan.

Ryan woke up to find her weeping. They dressed and went down to breakfast. There was a distance between them now. A sadness. Tom tried to get her to think forward to the time when it was all over, they would be together. She said nothing. Then in a quiet voice she said she would do what he asked. She would arrange a meeting with Bansan. No, he shouldn't be there, this she would do by herself. It was a Japanese matter, between Japanese. Soon, yes soon. She would fax Japan when she got back to Dublin. She thought Bansan might be coming to London next week. The fact that she was so familiar with where Bansan would be next week stung him, reminding him of the closeness of the continuing relationship between Kara and Bansan. It hurt him to be confronted so directly with this factor in their lives. Yes, she would go and see Bansan. Talk with him, give him the documents. Bansan would know what to do. Yes, she was sure he would do it. They parted at Frankfurt airport, looking at each other across a gap of strangeness, wanting to be close, unable.

On the flight back to the States, Tom Ryan went over it all

again, knowing that the deal was only possible because of Kara, that the Japanese business network is a maze of personal contacts where everyone knows everyone he is dealing with and everyone must be reliable, commitments must be fulfilled. There must be total confidence between the parties, built up over years, there was no access to this without Kara, to the closely layered relationships existing within the entire business framework. An exclusive club that no Westerner can ever expect to be a part of. It simply can't happen, the whole cultural complexity, the years of service, this society is not accessible to Westerners. They can never have a status comparable to any Japanese in the eyes of another Japanese. The business relationship of one Japanese to another will always be more important. Only through Kara's long-standing relationship with Bansan could the deal be set up in the available time.

\*     \*     \*

Kara knew all this too and that the prompt agreement between the parties concerned with the deal would mark the power and respect in which Bansan was held by his contacts and his seniority in the large business group surrounding him. When she met him in London, Bansan already knew this was a strange request. This could not be something coming out of the normal range of business contacts Kara made in Dublin. She had introduced him to many business deals in the past, generally small matters of helping here and taking a favour there. She had helped him with his Japanese contacts who wished to set-up manufacturing plants in Europe to gain access to the single market that was the new Europe. And of course, she had contacts with Government agencies and provided other local information for him about Ireland. But this was quite different.

Bansan looked at her and he then also knew for sure that this was not simply business, it had to have a personal dimension for her. She tried to be her usual bright self, but he could feel her discomfort. So, it did not matter. He valued her, had protected her, had loved her in some fashion over the lonely years travelling on business. She needed this favour for something else in her life. He thought it had to be a man, a special man. So be it. It was a part of her life that was not his concern. He would help her and it looked like the deal could be very profitable. His close business contacts with Japanese Organized Crime, the Yakuza, could be relied on to take care of matters on the ground.

The documents she handed to him described the device in a brief introduction. Then said why it was commercially so important and listed the Japanese companies who would be interested. Then the technical details and specification, some data showing performance. And the price for one unit on delivery, the unit to be delivered to him in the United States. The price was half a million US dollars, transferred to a Swiss bank account in advance, confirmed irrevocable bearer authorization on the account to be handed over in exchange for the device. Account details and copy letter to be provided one week ahead of the transaction for verification. All this to be supplied to a Post Office Box in California together with a contact phone number in New Orleans to arrange the hand over.

"Alright Kara, I will set up the deal, I am sure the information here is correct and so I am sure there will be a buyer, just as the documents say. There is not much time, but my colleagues will accept my word and proceed without the usual checks on doing this type of business with a Westerner."

"Thank you Bansan, you are most kind."

They took a taxi to the expensive Japanese restaurant he liked. No holding hands, no soft touches, no kisses, his was the formal Japanese way. He talked to her about where he had been recently. That he had bought a small island where he would retire soon and that he wanted her to live with him. As he had aged, his ugliness had diminished in the softening affects of age on his face. He now looked more old and tired than ugly.

That night she rubbed the aphrodisiac he used into him. But now she could not rid her mind of the sadness and complexity of her life. Two worlds had met, confronted each other, questioned her pragmatic policies, her attempts to simplify and separate. She felt like a whore making love. But she knew it would pass, like everything else. Nothing lasts.

# Chapter 15

From Frankfurt, Tom Ryan made his way back to the relative security of his hiding place in Mount Abraham. The next stages of the plan Jim had drawn up would proceed without him. The players now were Kara and Jim Ryan. He could only wait and hope now.

Mount Abraham was very much better than any hotel. It provided a superb standard of opulent comfort for it's "guests". Looking at the inhabitants helped keep Tom Ryan occupied for the first few days, he had never come across such a collection of very rich and very odd people. Some of the inhabitants, he decided, were simply there because they could afford to be odd and liked to be indulged. He assumed that somewhere in the expanse of buildings there were others who were more seriously off the rails. But the place was so spacious and, with a suite of his own, he wasn't bothered too much by contact with other patients. To preserve his anonymity, he generally kept to himself. Officially he was there as an alcoholic and his name was Jack Riordan. He reckoned that a substantial portion of those there were using assumed names, in any event, no one seemed to pay too much attention to his ancestry. He re-invented a past life as necessary and to occupy his time he read, walked in the beautiful grounds and talked nonsense with the psychologist about his drinking problem. But the days were long and it left too much time, time to think and worry about what was happening in Ireland and the plans O'Sullivan and the IRA were making for him. In his more depressed moments he thought it was possible that his death was already arranged, possible that a hit squad was already on it's way after him.

After a while, the institutional nature of the place, beautiful though it was, got to him, perhaps because of the secrets he had to keep, the fact that he was confined and in danger, it started to bring back unhappy echoes from his time in prison. Jim, it had been agreed, would only visit him or contact him strictly as necessary. It was, as Tom fully realized, the only way to improve security for them all, but the feelings of isolation, loneliness, powerlessness all only heightened the sense of imprisonment, of life slipping away in inactivity. But this imprisonment, this forced inactivity was set against a background of time passing, of the net closing around him, of death coming after him.

He was lying on his bed, staring up at the ceiling one afternoon, the sun streaming through the window of his room when the phone rang and startled him, he didn't get calls. It was the receptionist,
"Mr. Riordan, you have a visitor, will I direct him to your room?"

"Oh, I wasn't expecting anyone. Who is it?"

"It's a Mr. Kevin Ryan, he says you know him."

Jim's son, Kevin, that was odd, what was he doing here he wondered,
"Yeah, OK, send him down to my room."

When Kevin entered the room, he was surprised to find Tom standing against the wall, behind the door, as he pushed it open. To Kevin, Tom seemed tense and a little out of breath as he smilingly greeted his nephew, it was like Tom was a kid who had been caught with his fingers in the cookie jar.

Tom tried to cover the difficult situation, but he found himself awkwardly fumbling over his words and becoming even more ridiculous,
"Ah, Kevin, it's good to see you! So, you've come to see your old alcoholic uncle! Well, I'm glad of that, it's beginning to get lonely out here, nice and all as the place is. It's also nice to see someone normal for a change!"

With a clarity only possessed by the young, Kevin said, "Whatever else you are, I'm sure you are not alcoholic!"

"No I suppose that's one of life's blessings for me! So how about the two of us non-alcoholics going to get some coffee in the Coffee Shop they have here?"

"I'd rather sit here with you for a while and talk about something nearer to why you may actually be here, if that's OK with you?"

"What has your father told you?"

"Not much, as usual. But I figure it's got to be something to do with the IRA. Anyway, Dad is in New Orleans on business, an annual trade show or something. He's always busy."

"Umm."

"I don't want to know anything about it, well, at least not about the specific reason for you being here."

"Well, good! The less you know about it the better. And please, don't tell anyone that I'm here, that really is most important. I can't emphasize it enough."

"Yeah, I know, Dad has already given me the lecture about that, how it would affect your career being in for alcoholic treatment."

"OK, I know you're smart and it seems you've probably put two and two together, but you have to stay out of this and stay quiet about my being here. I'm very serious about that. Now, how are you doing at College? You must be nearly finished your computer course now?"

"College is fine and I'm finished in a few months time. That's no problem, but I would like you to talk to me, generally, about Ireland and the Troubles."

"You would be better talking to Jim."

"You know he won't talk about it at all, even with the present cease-fire. He just says he never thought he'd see the day when there would be peace and hopes it will last. Otherwise he wants to push it away, doesn't want to know. So I want you to talk to me about it. I have to understand."

"Understanding, now that's a big task you're setting me. I'm not sure anyone understands. I don't understand."

The absurdity, impossibility of trying to explain the past in Ireland, even if he limited it to his own lifetime, to this kid who had grown up in California! Kid, no, that was the first ridiculous thing. When he was Kevin's age he was nearing the end of his prison sentence in Belfast. But how could you explain Ireland in the Fifties to Kevin? Perhaps it was the boredom of his long days at Mount Abraham that encouraged him to even try and freed him of his normal reticence on the subject,
"So go on, what do you need to know?"

"Well, I suppose the first thing is the whole question of violence. Why does this supposedly Christian country engage in violence? You know, when you look at Gandhi

in India, where freedom from the British was obtained
without violence?"

"First the situation in India was very different, the British
were just about ready to get out. The idea of shedding colonies was not so difficult at that time. They had already
had the experience of Ireland nearly thirty years earlier. In
any event, even Gandhi couldn't stop the violence erupting
in India. The violence between the Moslems and the
Hindus was what brought about the division of India and
the creation of Pakistan."

"Yes, but why couldn't it have been tried in Ireland, the
use of passive resistance rather than killing?"

"The absolute answer is yes, you're right. And it would
have been fundamentally better all round. For all the same
basic reasons that Gandhi followed that course. But, in a
way, I suppose it had already been tried in Ireland. With
O'Connell, Parnell and so on. And it had failed for one
reason or another. And of course, the violence of 1916 was
seen as ultimately successful. The blood sacrifice and a
glorification of death for the cause of Irish Freedom. Martyrs whose deaths served to rouse the mass of the people."
Christ, he was coming out with all the old crap that had
blighted his school days. Talking with that damn psychologist must be affecting him after all. But there was no

escape, Kevin was determined to go on, seeking logical, reasonable answers,

"But times had changed, why was it not tried again?"

Tom's annoyance with himself and the whole process he had got into with Kevin meant he answered more sharply than he intended,
"It was. In the Civil Rights Marches of 1969. But you know what happened then. They were crushed with violence."

"So you are saying that violence is the only way?"

"With the benefit of hindsight, I believe that I originally got into the IRA for all the wrong reasons. You know, when I was at school, no one mentioned Gandhi, there was no discussion of India as an alternative model. It was all about the glorious dead, the brave Fenian Men, the oppression of Catholic Gaelic Ireland. That was the kind of crap in circulation in my schoolboy days. The first layer that I had to peel back was in trying to understand the relationship between the Catholic Church and the Irish State. When I was growing up, the Catholic Church was presented as full square behind the State. In fact the Church had always stood for the status quo, been behind the established British State in Ireland. That required a subtle little bit of historical re-positioning. The Catholic Church always opposed the IRA and revolution of any kind in Ireland. They were not interested in revolution, social instability, questioning the Pillars of State. Any move along that road and you would never know what people might question next. Not that any social revolution came about anyway. It was purely political. Everything else went on as before or worse."

"So, are you saying that now you see the whole thing as a waste of time, a mis-directed attempt to change things in Ireland?"

Jesus, now he was being held accountable for his life by this bright-eyed kid,
"No, not entirely. There were a lot of things wrong. On the whole, Ireland is better as a separate State. The British had caused far too many problems, Ireland was always something of a political plaything. An historical source of potential danger as a base from which their rivals could launch attacks on them. Their continued presence in the North could be described as a simple classic colonial situation. If the Catholics were black and the Protestants white, the similarities with the former British colonies in Africa would be obvious and I don't believe the modern world would tolerate it continuing."

"So what's the solution? Do you see the present negotiations succeeding, what will happen?"

"I really don't know. The problem is so intractable that it's hard to know what in realistic terms can be done. You can say that the two sides have to reach an understanding, an accommodation of some sort, learn to live together in a civilized way. But they are fundamentally so far from that and the situation is so easily inflamed, that it is hard to see a way forward. But the British have to say they are going. In some kind of orderly fashion, not withdrawing all connection or support. But they do have to get out, there has to be a fundamental change in the set-up. The basic problem, which won't go away, is that Northern Ireland is not a democratic state in any meaningful sense of the word. It was never intended to be. Until that basic fact is changed, there will be no peace."

"So at the end of the day it's Brits Out?"

Tom felt himself becoming impatient again, uneasy with all this,
"Look, I don't feel comfortable with such simple notions anymore, but that's certainly part of it. It's got to stop being a colony. It's hard though to see the usual postcolonial situation arising there, you know, where the colonists either accept a new situation or go home. Like in Rhodesia some years ago or South Africa now. Perhaps in the case of Northern Ireland because of the very closeness of the homeland. They aren't going to move. And at the same time they aren't going to accept they are not at home."

"So, do you regret having been a part of the IRA, the armed struggle?"

"Regret, I'm not sure if you can talk about regret for the past, you have to look at the circumstances of the time. I still see a continuing political problem that needs a solution. Certainly I regret the awful violence of the last twenty-five years. If there was another course I would chose it. When I first joined the IRA, I did it for all the wrong reasons. Well perhaps that's not right. Perhaps I should say that I didn't know all the factors in the situation, but then, I suppose you never know all the factors in any situation in life. Unfortunately, we all go forward on incomplete information, incomplete understanding. The second time I got involved, I did know more, a lot more, but I was presented with an outrage. I had to respond, not let it go, do nothing. The rest followed as a consequence. Yes, I regret in the sense that I wish there was another way."

"But now we're back to what I said earlier, the bottom line is that the British will only respond to violence or the treat of violence?"

"You can certainly argue that is what history teaches, all around the world. The only hope I have is that the south of Ireland, the Republic, most of the country if you like, is so peaceful. That may seem a strange thing to say. But when you think of the history of Ireland, the amazing thing is not that there is violence in the North, but that the rest of the country has become so peaceful. Perhaps the North can be brought back from all of this, can find a peaceful future. But it needs to be soon, the longer this goes on for, the more social damage that is done. The more psychopaths we will have left over on both sides. The basis for a whole continuing criminal empire is being created."

"Like the Mafia? Surely that could never happen? The IRA are fighting for their rights."

"Yes, but it could end up just like the Mafia."

He looked at Kevin and wondered just what the hell was all this about? The entire conversation left him feeling deeply disturbed, irritated with himself and with Kevin,
"You stay out of it anyway. It's not your problem, you're an American. You get your degree in Computer Science and the world is out there waiting for you. Enjoy the good things that this world gives. Do something constructive and useful. The ancient evil of the North of Ireland just consumes all those who get involved. Find someone to love, have children, make friends! Enjoy life! You know it's really very short, time passes quickly, ever more quickly as you get older. We have to select what we want in life. Select things which are good and which will sustain you, positive things. Like your father."

"Yeah, I know, Jim keeps telling me."

"Now, how about some coffee?"

Tom walked with Kevin to the Coffee Shop Restaurant and the chance to change the atmosphere and move the conversation on to more general and mundane aspects of life, hoping to talk about his studies, girlfriends, sports, other interests, anything but the IRA. After a while they left and walked through the maze of the corridors toward the entrance area. Tom stopped short of entering the main entrance area with its glass frontage which could be observed from the car park.

Walking back to his own room, Tom felt uneasy after this visit that should have been so easy and enjoyable. He liked Kevin and had given him an honest, uncalculated response. The kind of discursive discussion you might have with any dis-interested party. Perhaps he should have painted a starker picture. The car bombs, the assassinations, the reality and fear of brutal violence and what it does to people's lives. The reality of innocent people with their bodies torn apart after a car bomb. Blood, brains, limbs and bone blasted and scattered all over a street.

Perhaps Kevin was just a disinterested party. Dear God, he hoped he was and would stay out of it. This family had paid the price of his own youthful romance with the IRA. That was more than enough. Surely it couldn't happen again. Dear God, No! He didn't want to think about the awful prospect that now confronted him, Kevin becoming involved in the IRA. He felt he'd been caught off guard, not expecting such a conversation in this place, never expecting Kevin to show an interest in the IRA. He wished now that he had been more careful. Damn it, why hadn't Jim talked to Kevin, why was it left to him here and now of all times, to "explain"? He thought you couldn't opt out, it didn't matter what your views were, you couldn't opt out and just leave it. Jim should have talked to Kevin before now. But Jim was in New Orleans and that was the next stage of the plan.

# Chapter 16

While Tom Ryan was talking Irish Politics to Kevin Ryan in Mount Abraham, Jim Ryan was already in New Orleans. This was to be the venue for the next stage of the plan devised by Jim Ryan. A robbery in New Orleans.

New Orleans in early March, the week after Mardi-Gras. Already warming in pleasant contrast to the still frozen northern cities. Mardi-Gras with its noisy, colourful, all night street parades and drunks from everywhere. Filling the hotels and bringing early season tourist money into the city. But now the city had put on it's business front. Hosting an enormous convention, an even bigger money-spinner. The 1995 Pittsburgh Conference and Exposition.

By far the largest exhibition anywhere in the world dedicated solely to advanced scientific instrumentation. Bringing in tens of thousands of conferees, the chemists who used the instrumentation in their research programs. From every major university, every government department dealing with everything from environment to weapons research and from every kind of industry they came. If it was new, it was here, the conference and exhibition defined the state of the art in this area of science. Every hotel room had sold out months before. At 5pm on Wednesday evening, March

8, the elaborate Riverside Convention Center closed after the third busy exhibition day. The wide exits jammed with an enormous disgorging mass of people, mostly heading back to their hotels. Some chose to walk despite their tired legs and aching feet, talking with friends and colleagues, others joined a line for one of the stream of Conference supplied shuttle buses.

The endless carpeted exhibit aisles were now deserted. The billions of dollars of instrumentation left idle in the lavish colourful displays. The simultaneous multi-location scientific presentations had stopped. The business day had concluded. Only Jim Ryan knew that to-morrow would be different. The Pittsburgh Conference would never be the same again. That was one of the few things he could be sure of.

Late evening, darkness now enclosing the still warm city. Inviting the visitors to the interior of Crescent City, Land of Dreams. Across from the bright lights of the French Quarter, the other side of Canal Street, on the thirty-second floor of the Sheraton, Jim Ryan got ready to leave his hotel suite. He had dressed carefully in his expensive casual clothes. It could have been just another night for him in this city. If it wasn't for the tight grip of fear in his stomach and the tiny ultra-sensitive x-ray detector that now lay on the shelf in his bathroom. He had just stolen it.

The only one in the world. The basic technology had been developed by a smaller specialist corporation, who had received funding as part of a military sponsored research program. This version had just been cleared for limited commercial release. The business implications were enormous. Every other instrument in this field was now obsolete. A fact that the main competitive corporations were only too well aware of. In the last few months, the news of its forthcoming introduction and the inevitable consequences had reverberated around the world from California to Japan.

Dr. Jim Ryan, Vice President of Marketing for the vast international Parker-Wotton Corporation. He too had realized the implications and convinced the corporation to move swiftly with a takeover bid for the cash starved Midon Corporation. The deal would not be announced for some little time, but the technology was secured for the USA. Dr. J. Aldrich Parker had insisted on this. Some behind the scenes government pressure had also been applied to Midon. The reality of being funded by military sponsored research was made clear to them.

The modern scientific instrument business had developed in the USA from almost nothing in the period following the Second World War. It came from the war-based development of modern electronics and the military interest in infrared, microwaves, and all that science could do. The war had ensured that the military were totally converted to the power technology could provide. Despite the bland appearance of the scientific instrument business, underlying it was a strong continuing connection to military related research and the space program. The result was that major American instrument corporations developed rapidly and dominated the business.

The Europeans had some companies active in the field and the Americans had put subsidiaries into Europe. But the Europeans were behind in technology and marketing power because, until the recent single European Market, they simply didn't have the market scale necessary to vitalize their business. Even now they couldn't really compete against the USA with a truly European based company. The Japanese had adopted a different approach. They had identified this as a business they wanted a piece of. It was worthwhile, had a future and although not like the big markets for cars and consumer electronics which they already dominated, they needed these newer specialized smaller markets for new growth and opportunities.

The Presidents of the most powerful of the US corporations were determined to keep this as a US owned and run business. They were fighting back and as far as J. Aldrich Parker was concerned, Japan was definitely not going to get this latest piece of US developed technology. His acquisition of the Midon Corporation would see to that. All was well. Everyone was happy. The close and long standing relationship between the Parker-Wotton Corporation and the US Government had ensured the right result.

Now Jim Ryan had stolen the only working, commercial version of the device, just a few hours earlier. Right out of the massive Electron Microscope on the Midon exhibition booth. The respected, go-ahead, trusted friend and advisor of J. Aldrich Parker. A thief. Only hours before certain discovery.

The detector was less than the size of his thumb. Mounted in its advanced package of electronics, it looked like a computer chip. By buying a pair of earrings for his wife, he had obtained a small thin gift box in the hotel shopping area that morning. Now he put the detector into the box. Taped the box securely and then taped the box into his inside jacket pocket. It was time to go.

In the hotel elevator, the box seemed to burn its small hard rectangular outline into his chest. Out through the vast glitzy hotel lobby. A black middle aged pianist, dinner jacket and grand piano, gently playing jazz standards for the customers in the lobby bar. Now it was Gershwin's "Summertime". Smooth and easy. As he walked through the lobby, he wondered if this tune brought back memories for everyone? But it was a different kind of jazz he would hear shortly, away from the plush comfort and security of the big hotel.

Across the broad width of Canal Street, careful of the streetcars. Into the French Quarter. Narrow criss-crossing streets with old low sized brick buildings. Wrought iron balconies. A different world. Not at all like a typical North American city. This had a different feel to it. A sense of historical closeness to France and Spain, the Cajun influence, slavery, the heat of a deep southern summer, jazz and prostitution.

Walk down Bourbon Street. Restaurants and bars. All busy with life. Passing splashes of bright light and sound. People enjoying their evening out on the town. Some standing, drinks in their hands, on the small balconies above street level. Others crowding the street with their slow wanderings. The sound of people in excited talk fought against the sounds of traditional style jazz and the blues, all filling the street with life. Conflicting tunes and forms battling for attention. Packaged entertainment. Take your time. Try to enjoy the atmosphere again. Why not. There was no rush now. Try to stay calm and behave normally. He had planned to be very early for this meeting.

A good-looking hooker standing in a doorway. She noticed him. Yes, a definite prospect, a well-dressed lone man. Slim, fit, not showing his years. Good strong features.

Lightly tanned. Carefully styled hair, just a touch of grey.
A look of hardness too in the eyes.

Despite everything that was pounding through his mind, he
found he was looking at her. Early twenties, finely struc-
tured light Creole face, long black hair. Her white dress,
tight into her body. But strange, how she seemed to glow.
It was like she was translucent. Unreal. A shimmering dre-
amlike image of beauty. Christ, he thought, the tension
playing games with my mind. But for the few seconds
between seeing and passing her, he stared, aware of the
mis-timed absurdity of the feelings of intense, wondrous
desire she aroused in him. As he came close, she smiled,

"Hi there, and how are you doin' to-night?"

He thought of the attractions of this alternative evening she
was offering. So much easier than the complex and horrible
reality in which he now found himself. Perhaps another
time. It would be nice to have nothing else to think about.
Like so many easy nights before. He passed by, said
nothing in response to her come on. Now the lights diminished as he walked further. The tourists were being left
behind. He was entering the darker side of New Orleans,
the far side of Esplanade Avenue.

It was 11pm. The jazz joint was in a dark, narrow street. It
was like a run-down old style shop without the shop contents and without the fittings. A thin, tall, gangly black guy

on the door. Age indeterminate. Cigarette hanging from his mouth.

"Five dollars". Nothing else was said. But Ryan became keenly aware of his contrasting whiteness. The band was just getting started. Still only a few customers. All black. Mainly standing. A few tables and chairs in the back. He wondered what the place would look like in cold hard daylight. No doubt even more rundown. In this limited light, the interior seemed a combination of slate black and dark brown. Just some forlorn coloured lights strung from the column supported ceiling, half-heartedly trying to brighten their way through the smoke and dust laden air. It all looked like it had just been brought into a temporary existence. A basic bar was to the right and just up from the entrance door. The bar was a functional counter, set in front of the wall shelved with bottles and glasses. Opposite was a raised area for the band. The young black kid playing tenor sax fronted a group of older guys. The light caught the gold of the sax and sent a darting flickering glitter out as the kid moved. Exuding an easy sensuality, the instrument and he were as one. He played the blues in a straight line to Charlie Parker, dead long before the kid was born. Now the deep rich mellow tones filled the whole space. Seductive, lonely with all the emotion of eternal irreconcilable loss. Smooth then raw again as the kid took his improvisation way into the upper end of the altissimo range. The emotions released by the sax only echoed the atmosphere of tension and uneasy excitement. Anything could happen here. It was off the edge of mainstream society.

The respectable ordered society that Jim Ryan had claimed as his. With his chemistry Ph.D., his expensive clothes, his responsible job with the Parker-Wotton Corporation, his beautiful home in California. Complete with Ellen and the kids. The social life they had cultivated. Here he was, now a thief. His plan had seemed so clean-cut and simple, but the sweaty reality was different. Life for everyone around him becoming impossibly complicated and dangerous. With a piece of advanced technology which was only just off the top-secret list. All hell was going to break loose once the theft was discovered. But there was no going back, he was locked in now.

Here anxiously waiting, on the wrong side of town making a desperate effort to control the mad rushing cascade of events. How, he wondered, had it all come to this? The threads of the past, entwining him, not letting him escape. After all the years of change and a new country, a new life. Pulled back to a time and place he had tried to contain and bury in the recesses of his mind.

After a rising crescendo, the sax kicked out with a resonant low B. In the sudden silence, the note reverberated within him and he could again feel the small box tight against his chest.

# Chapter 17

There was some applause from the still small crowd. The band talked and joked between themselves. Jim Ryan remembered it, those breaks between numbers. Playing at dances back in Dublin while he went through College, how it had been an escape. How in another life he might have been a professional musician, but he had rejected that choice, opted for security and stability and a career.

The roots of the predicament he now found himself in went to a much earlier time. Born into it was perhaps the only way to describe it. But not directly, he had what seemed like every possibility in life. Yet it had a sort of inevitability about it, right from the start in school. That was how it started for him at least, and of course, more particularly for his brother, Tom. Jesus, what a waste of a life. The past, remote in time and space had brought even Jim back from his carefully cultivated existence, back into its destructive web. He had spent his life trying to escape by building a new life, fashioned how he wanted it, now he felt a resentful anger build in him as the past reclaimed him.

He could remember clearly that first school day at St. Brendan's. One of those seminal points in life. Even though the sun shone brightly, the regimented granite buildings with their tall windows looked frightening to him. Overpowering greyness. The carefully maintained, but flowerless grounds. A world without joy.

His father had come with him. His father was a senior civil servant in the Department of Finance, who had also been a student at St. Brendan's and was a classmate of some who were now teachers. To-day he returned, bringing with him his second son, to meet his old friend Brother John Ignatius O'Reilly. His father dressed in the conservative style of civil servants everywhere, even carried a rolled umbrella along with his old style brief case. His hours were regular, his life ordered and careful. His solid red brick house, quiet and well maintained, a basis from which he could expect his two sons to do well. As was normal with such families and in that time, the sons were sent to schools run by the religious.

In this case the Christian Brothers, not very far up on the scale of religious distinction in education, not like the Jesuits or the Benedictines. The Christian Brothers, dressed in forbidding black, this religious order provided strictly and brutally enforced discipline as a first priority for the sons of the middle classes. And a basic learnt education where not too many questions would be welcome. Don't stray outside the given truth of a reactionary Irish Catholic Church. And of course, a strong crude sense of Irish nationality was instilled into all.

Based on a selective view of history, turning on a revolution which failed miserably as a military operation but went on to make martyrs for the cause of Irish Freedom. The principal organizers of the 1916 revolution could be described as poets, teachers, trade unionists and general dreamers. The eventual success of their efforts must surely have come as a complete surprise to them and left them with the unexpected problem of what to do then. A history had to be written which justified them and defined the new State. And the heart of the history was to be Gaelic, all other historical influences were simply "invaders". The fact that the Celts were themselves invaders who had destroyed a previous advanced culture was not mentioned. Neither was the fact that just about all of the population of the country must have had a diverse mixture of blood lines from Vikings to English.

He had started to wonder about this as he watched the teachers invent Gaelic versions of names for those whose names weren't "Irish". The absurdity of it, why weren't their actual names acceptable? The school register only contained "Irish" names and "Irish" versions of names. Ryan was, of course, alright, but kids with names like Banville, Lambert or Stafford, were transformed out of all recognition. This was a first lesson from the new State for it's young citizens, you had to be Irish and that meant being Gaelic. Even your name would be changed by it's officials as they thought fit.

But hostile views were not welcome in the newly written history as taught by the Christian Brothers and other pillars of the new State. Forty years after the revolution, the new Ireland was still unsure of itself. There was still trouble with the British over the northern piece of the island still under British rule. A festering problem with no solution and which generated countless spin-off problems.

In the late 1950's, Ireland was still a country isolated and turned in on itself, cut off from the mainstream and poor. While most of the world enjoyed a post war economic boom, Ireland had it's own private economic recession, self-inflicted by the ultra conservative financial management of the Department of Finance. The result was a massive wave of emigration, disrupting families, de-populating entire regions, sending ill educated and ill-equipped young men and women from farms to the big cities of Britain, the USA and Canada. This was the Ireland in which the two brothers grew up, but they were shielded by their middle class, solid and secure background from the day-to-day economic realities that faced most of the population. A security which was to be torn apart within a few years.

Tom was the older by three years. Already well established and well regarded at St. Brendan's. Now Jim and his father walked the long corridor from the massive main entrance to Brother O'Reilly's office. The young Brother who had first received them knocked on the office door.

"Come!" and they were admitted to a large room furnished with a massive desk that seemed enormous to young Jim. On the wall behind the desk was a large stark black crucifix with an agonized bleached white Christ dripping bright red painted blood. A frightening, awful and overpowering image of agonized death. As the horrific vision came back into his mind, he was struck by the parallel between Ireland and New Orleans which had it's own vivid religious statuary around the town and the link from there to the lurid images of Voodoo brought from Africa and Irelands pre-Christian paganism. He shivered and recoiled from the barbarity with the remembered mind of his childhood.

After the formality of the introduction of him as "James" to the Headmaster who was referred to by his father as "Brother O'Reilly", Jim was then ignored while the two former classmates talked as old friends. Talked of the others who had been with them in school, where were they now and how well they had done in life, when they had last been seen, old memories of sporting achievements, and did you know.... Then the state of the country and the economic outlook. Here his father was the visiting expert, to be listened to with close attention and respect.

The whole school environment was intensely and exclusively male and the forcefulness and underlying brutality of this male world became apparent to the young boy. In contrast with his earlier school years in the convent school.

There the atmosphere had been entirely female and Jim
was the darling of the nuns. Now it was all totally different,
a different smell to this rough separated world of male celibacy. A different feeling from this artificial masculine
enclave where life was defined in terms of sporting success
and academic achievement. Even the friendship between
his father and the headmaster left Jim uneasy in this new
overbearing environment.

But this was to be a training ground for him, where the arts
of an easy charm, a quick witted intelligence, a little well
measured deceit, all allowed him to thrive in this little
closed-in world he despised, developing the diverse abilities
he would later use to excel in corporate life. The school
unwittingly gave him an excellent preparation for life, just
as Brother O'Reilly had assured his father they would,

"Isn't it only to be expected, isn't he Tom's young brother,
we'll expect great things from him and I'm sure we won't
be disappointed!"

Indeed they weren't disappointed. But then Jim Ryan took
good care that they never got close to him. His smooth
passage through St. Brendan's largely avoided the ritual
brutality administered as a matter of course to those who
did not perform and conform to expectations. The empha-
sis on a stultifying religion and on the violent politics of
the country rolled off him. His questioning of the accepted

dogmas of religion and politics were taken as interesting academic exercises by a bright boy who excelled at mathematics and science. The fact that he might actually have believed in the wild ideas he put forward was ridiculous. Wasn't he Tom's brother? And they all knew Tom. And of course, his father. All sound.

Tom was different. The two brothers had a closeness that was only enhanced by their natural differences. Tom's interest was languages. And religion and politics. All of these interests were carefully channelled for him at St. Brendan's. And he was good at sports. Ideal material for the non-practical academic basis of St. Brendan's.

Tom was 14 years old when he joined the youth section of the IRA. His parents thought he had joined a scouting organization for boys. Winter weekends camping in the Dublin Mountains, patriotic songs of historic freedom fighters and oppression by the English. Cold to the bone, wet and miserable, all endured for the rightful just cause of Irish Freedom. Jim was the only one in the family to know what Tom was really doing.

Three years later, on a wet and cold November night, Tom was half dead in a field in Northern Ireland and the news of his capture and subsequent trial was all over the newspapers and the quiet, respectable Ryan family was catapulted into trauma.

Only now, in a sleazy bar on the outskirts of New Orleans, the old trauma was re-emerging into a different life as Jim waited for the Japanese to arrive and do the deal he had set-up to save his brother Tom. An attempt to stop it all escalating and reaching back to Dublin and their parents. His mind continued to wander through the past, now bringing him back to how it had been, when he was sixteen and with Hazel. He thought again how they were all trapped and entwined and could only hope to at least gain some kind of damage limitation by committing this exercise in madness. Even he, who prided himself in his positive, optimistic view of life, began to wonder in the darkness of the bar how it could end differently from how it all began. He was still locked-in by having escaped from the world he found intolerable, locked-in by guilt in having escaped, wanting to make it all right for those he had left behind. He knew only that he would try this, this one further turn of the wheel, but his mind insisted that the cast of players had remained the same, the script would just unfold. Relentlessly trying to pull him back into what he had tried to escape from, it seemed to him now as though an evil force of destruction was at work, it would fight his attempts to create another world, it would threaten to overwhelm him. The music pumped out it's rhythmic jazz beat, the sax smooth and lush, but it just sounded like a discordant noise to him now as he waited. He thought of Brother O'Reilly and the Mathematics class when O'Reilly had held him up to ridicule by announcing to the entire class that Jim Ryan, his star pupil, solved problems like a farmer with a bull in a field which had two gates and how the farmer closed one gate with the greatest care, leaving the other wide open. He hoped he had closed both gates this time. It had seemed straightforward when he first thought of this plan as a solution and spoken with Tom in Mount Abraham. He wondered if his sense of problem solving and being able to solve problems no matter what they were had maybe run away with him. It looked frighteningly dangerous now, alone in this bar.

# Chapter 18

Wednesday night, March 8, 1995, Bansan with his colleagues and the two members of the Yakuza went to eat in the small Japanese restaurant off Charles Avenue in New Orleans. Bansan had done the deal for the equivalent of 2.5 million dollars. After expenses, this would leave an excellent profit margin, even for a high-risk venture like this.

The simple restaurant was crowded as the Japanese group ate and drank, the small square tables packed close together. Three tables had been joined to facilitate the booking made by the Japanese group. Bansan had a central position along one side of the enlarged table. As they ate their main course of Sashimi, they noisily slurped the Miso soup from their raised soup bowls allowing air to enter their mouths along with the soup to experience the full taste of the delicate flavour. The noisy eating habits of the Japanese men attracted disapproving looks from the Americans sitting at the next table, one of whom blew his nose vigorously into his handkerchief. The Japanese group in their turn discussed the extraordinary ignorance of so many Westerners in general and Americans in particular and the poor quality of service to be found in the Banks, in the dirty condition of the taxi cabs, inadequate airport information and the many other unfavourable comparisons with modern Japan.

They all agreed that it was hard to believe that America was still the most powerful country in the world.

Another round of hot Sake was ordered. The two Yakuza, with quick repeated nodding and bowing head movements, politely asked to be excused the fourth round of drinks for business reasons. This was agreed by Bansan, after all, business was the purpose of their group. Everyone acknowledged him as the senior man, respect was shown. But the meal was a group occasion, to relax and mark their togetherness in this venture. A visit to one of the exotic local brothels had been arranged for 10.00pm. Over the meal they cheerfully discussed the reports they had heard of the many services available, the beauty of the girls, the different ethnic types to choose from. They were enjoying the prospect of availing of one of New Orleans great claims to fame. They all went together of course, all part of the ritual of being together, of sharing the same objectives. The two Yakuza would complete the business transaction at about 1am and return directly to Bansan's suite at the Hilton with the instrument part. To facilitate matters, the Hamanoshi Corporation had made available one of its block-booked hotel suites to Bansan and his colleagues. Bansan would personally bring the device back to Japan, taking the first flight out of New Orleans on Thursday morning.

As the two Yakuza stepped out of the taxi outside the run-down nightspot on the wrong side of town, they could already hear the music pouring into the street. They told the taxi driver to wait, they would not be long. The club doorman lazed back against one side of the door. The thinner, taller of the Yakuza smiled and asked if they might come in.

"Twenty dollars", he replied using his stern, serious voice, these muthers could contribute ten to his personal fund. Funny looking fuckers though, just look at the hands on that one, like he had been in some kind of accident or had some kind of arthritis, all big knuckles. No, that was one dude you wouldn't fuck with. No sir, that muther had real fuckin' physical presence, fuckin' death walkin' on two legs.

The two Japanese went over to the bar, got themselves drinks and surveyed the place. It was getting full now. All black except for the one white man standing at the bar. They looked across curiously at the band which was really getting into the music as the night went on and the band relaxed and the instruments warmed up. The crowd appreciatively shouted their approval after each solo. Customers moving with tight, quick little movements to the music, swinging their shoulders, rubbing up against each other. Laughing, giving each other the come on. The social interactions revolved around sex and drugs. Flashily dressed guys making moves on sexy looking women. Laughing and gesticulating, they all looked like they were enjoying themselves and each other.

The doorman came over to the older man behind the bar. His thin sprawling limbs seeming to go in disconnected directions as he moved. As he spoke to the barman, his sentences were punctuated by a rasping laugh,

"Hey man, dis' is one crazy Wednesda' night in here, yeh? Ain' we jus' gettin' some real weird muthers in! Wha' yu' think that there honkys' be'n do'in in here? He be'n standin' at da bar for an hour or mor' now! Ain' pickin' ups no women! Too well dressed for yo' average tourist, not tha' we sees many up here's anyways. An' those last two muthers, they causes trouble an' I'm gon' outa here so fast!" He pulled a face in mock serious horror, his thin features became drawn and skeletal.

The large well-rounded barman reassured him,
"Yeh, yeh, ain' no sweat Rolando, jus' quieten down now, the boss don' mind whose money it is. Probably in for that big convention in town. They ain' doin' no harm and that makes a change for the customers in here!"

Rolando laughed a high pitched, coughing laugh, delighted at this interaction and brief respite from standing by himself at the door. The barman continued to busy himself filling drinks as fast as he could and Rolando went back to his door still laughing to himself, to await the next arrivals, his movements more or less following the beat of the music.

Jim Ryan had seen them come in. One taller and thinner,

the other like a walking block of granite. A very serious piece of muscle. But the thin guy, even with the glasses, looked like he could take care of himself without any problem. Offer you a variety of recipes from his menu of methods of death. They saw him, nodded by lifting their heads slightly in his direction and picked up a drink at the bar. Then casually came over. The thinner one spoke,

"Nice place, you also Pittcon?"

"Yeah, I'm at Pittcon, just taking a few hours off, hear a little music and relax. Good to see you."

Their brief stilted conversation was almost drowned by the band in full swing, the music superimposed over the roomful of rival shouted conversations going on. That was no problem, it was all much as expected. Contact had been made. They waited for about five minutes, then the thinner of the Yakuza followed Jim to the Mens room. It was so small they could just about both get in. The smell was suffocating, reminding Jim of schooldays again. He could only imagine how disgusting the Japanese found it. But there was no facial expression to say so. Without a word, Ryan exchanged the little box for the envelope. The Japanese took the thin gift box and without smiling inquired,

"You mind I look?"

Ryan said "Not at all" and nodded to confirm approval.

The manufacturers identification was on the small chip and the part number, just like the picture the Yakuza had been shown and studied. Still absorbed and looking at the chip, he nodded his head and quietly grunted a satisfied long nasal "Ah". Ryan opened the envelope to check the original of the letter of authorization on the Swiss Bank. It all looked OK, just like the copy he had received, but this was the original complete with original ink signatures.

The Yakuza bowed slightly to the Geyshing,
"Thank you, Sir."

There was no honour to be shown, just a small cursory gesture, offensive in its insignificance as Ryan noted.

# Chapter 19

Gus Hartman was at his desk early on Thursday. He had been with the FBI in New Orleans for 15 years and the job was getting to him. When he joined the FBI, after getting out of the Army, he had been young, slim, fit and keen. His marriage was happy and solid and the move to New Orleans was full of hope. Now he was overweight, his clothes didn't fit him right, he didn't get enough exercise, smoked too much and his family life was going down the tubes. His stomach hurt and the over the counter remedy he carried with him wasn't working anymore. When he did get home, not only his wife, but now his kids also ignored him.

All this was translating itself into permanent war with the world. The paper work, the office politics, the budget, the job was one big pain in the neck. He had started to think he needed to get into something else, maybe join one of the private security firms. The pay might not be great, but the hours would be more regular. Anything had to be better than this.

It was 11.30am on Thursday, March 9, 1995 when he pulled himself out of the cab at the Riverside Convention Center. Cab was the only practical way to get there with the limited parking in the area,

"You need a receipt?"

"Yeah I need a receipt, Uncle Sam is real keen on receipts."

Fuck it, he thought, he was being used as cannon fodder, thrown in to stop a gap, ensure that some immediate action was seen to be taken. Ensure that Public Relations would have no problems. Cover your ass time for the FBI. The team from Washington wouldn't be here for three hours at least. The Washington team would take the credit as they always did when they were brought in and be sure to give him a hard time when they arrived all fresh and gung-ho. Meanwhile he had been pulled off the local job he had been working on for the past three weeks and he was sure as hell that his local operation would be totally fucked-up as a result.

He went through the entrance doors, under the banner sign. It read,
"Pittcon. '95, Stimulating the Minds of Today's and Tomorrow's Scientists."
He flashed ID at one of the security guards,
"Hartman, FBI, I'm here to see Dr Janet Balzer."

"Yes Sir, the Exposition Chairman is expecting you."

He was led through the vast carpeted entrance area and

downstairs to the subterranean complex of the Conference
Organizers Offices.

She was mid-forties he reckoned, attractive, good woman-
executive type clothes, nice legs, expensive blond hair,
bright, single, probably in some kind of relationship, didn't
smoke, exercised, had a good job and looked after herself.
One of the two guys with her in the office got up and said
he was Jack Drager from the FBI labs. Drager explained
he was a Conferee, just here like all the other punters, but
the Bureau had got a message to him via the Conference
to make himself available. Hartman knew this thing had
gone all the way to the top and back down again to end up
an hour later in his lap with Drager brought in for technical
advice. The other guy, low sized ultra-neat appearance and
with glasses, and looking like he was about to shit himself,
introduced himself as from the Parker-Wotton Corporation
and said his job at the show was Booth Manager with over-
all responsibility for the booth. His badge said he was
David Walther, Ph.D.

Walther explained that all the more senior corporate personnel with the exhibiting companies had already left, they
all had their flights out of New Orleans booked for the
previous night or first thing that morning. This was the last
day of the show and "tear down" of the exhibition was just
4 hours away. No one who could help it, he explained,
stayed around for the dog end last day of the show, or the

sweat and chaos of tearing down the exhibits and getting everything packed up and shipped out. Janet Balzer gave him a disapproving look, like she regarded all the days of the exhibition as equally valuable. But it seemed the theft had left Walther from Parker-Wotton seriously stressed and he didn't notice her at all. He had been left holding the baby and the baby was pissing all over him. Hartman ignored Drager and started in on Walther,
"So tell me what happened, I understand something has been stolen from your booth and there are National Security issues?"

Before Walther could respond, Janet Balzer interjected,
"Well first of all I should say, Mr Hartman, that nothing like this has ever happened at the Pittsburgh Conference before."

He looked at her wearily, that was as good a way as any of saying security was non-existent in any real sense. OK, he thought, we start with the fact that my ten-year-old kid could have walked in and taken out anything he could carry. Maybe she could sort out one puzzle for him,
"Yeah sure. So let me clear one thing first, why is this called the "Pittsburgh Conference" or "Pittcon" when it's in New Orleans?"

This was familiar territory for her,

"The Conference was started just after the war in Pittsburgh by a volunteer group of local scientists. It's still run by the successors of that group, but these days it is so big that it has to be held in major locations, like this."

Hartman turned his attention back to Walther,
"Right, now that I'm clear on that, can we go over and take a look at where the theft happened?"

As they walked through the vast exhibition space, down carpeted aisle after carpeted aisle, Hartman had never seen anything quite like it. Sure, he had been dragged to consumer appliance exhibitions with his wife, but the sheer quality of the displays, the vast amount of technology that seemed to be here, it was incredible. Not at all like what he remembered from the school chemistry lab. Unlike consumer exhibitions, here he noticed that the standard of dress of the visitors was remarkable. No one looked sloppy here. The whole thing reeked of quality. The average IQ and the average income must be well ahead of the national average and they were also damn near all white, well, maybe with the exception of the numerous Japanese who seemed to be running all around the place in little groups.

On the way over, Drager explained that he could be of little help, this X-Ray stuff wasn't his area of speciality, he was involved with "Chromatography". Hartman decided he

sure didn't need to know about "Chromatography", whatever the hell that was, what he needed to know about was
this X-Ray stuff,
"So, does the FBI lab have someone else here who is a
specialist in this X-Ray business?"

"No, not this year, trips like this are rationed out with the
budget limitations on staff costs these days. I haven't been
to this show in three years. Right now I should be attending
a scientific presentation in my own area. I'll do what I can
to fill you in, but the guys from Parker-Wotton will take
pretty good care of the technical stuff anyway."

"So, tell me," Hartman said turning to Walther, "what does
Parker-Wotton do and what is this X-Ray machine?"

Walther went into his sales spiel,
"Well first off we're the biggest instrument manufacturer
in the world. The Electron Microscope is a way of mapping
the elemental composition of materials. You only need a
very small fragment for analysis and our new model has an
X-Ray detector that is about a hundred times more sensitive and with much greater resolution than anything
before."

Hartman turned to Drager and raised his eyebrows slightly,
hoping for clarification,
"Well it's a way of finding out what a material is made from

in great detail and how the different chemical elements or compounds are distributed through the material. This kind of thing is important in a whole lot of areas, like examining the detailed structure of metals or metal components."

"You mean like after an air crash?"

"Yeah sure, and forensic type work is one thing it could be used for, but there are lots of other industrial type problems it's good for."

Hartman needed to get some idea of why it should have been stolen, so he turned to Walther again,
"OK, so I can see if this is a better widget, this detector, someone might want to steal it and maybe copy it. But don't you guys at Parker-Wotton have Patents and stuff to protect you?"

"You'd really need to ask Jim Ryan about that, but he's not here to-day."

"So who's this Jim Ryan?"

"He's our Senior Vice President of Marketing. He was responsible for the Midon buy-out when we got this technology and he'd know the patent position."

"OK, so he's not here and you'd better do the best you can to explain this to me."

Walther replied, some of the earlier tension in his voice easing just a little as they walked and he started to explain again, this time about the business,

"In general, the situation is we have all sorts of patents and they can be useful, but getting a patent depends on where you are. A thing like this is important to our competitors, including the Japanese and European companies. We might find we have problems in getting the patents through in such areas. Or the patent we eventually get through may be so watered down as to be damn near useless or easily gotten around. So, with new technology, we try to keep it away from the competition for as long as possible. Everyone in the business plays games, of course, like registering newly recruited staff as conferees and sending them around to exhibitor's booths to check out their stuff. Or recruiting staff from our competitors. It's a tough business now."

From what Hartman was seeing of the business as they walked through the aisles, it didn't look all that tough to him,

"OK, so stealing it might make sense to your competitors, but where's the National Security issue apart from the loss to Parker-Wotton?"

"The device has come out of military work the Midon Corporation has been involved with. We've recently bought Midon so that's how we're involved. The military are still sensitive about the technology, there are tight restrictions in place about export licences. The military are concerned about who gets to play with it for the next few years."

Hartman decided there must have been some powerful pressure applied to get this into the commercial area and over-rule the military interests,
"So it could be straight espionage, stolen for military use? Maybe even some terrorist type outfit?"

Walther seemed uncertain,
"It's possible, but I really have no idea about the military side."

They arrived at the Midon booth which was located beside the much bigger Parker-Wotton booth. Walther explained that next year the two booths would be fully integrated. The Electron Microscope was big. The only microscope Hartman had ever seen was the little desktop optical micro-scope kids used for looking at leaves and beetles legs. This thing stood over 6 feet tall and occupied a floor area the size of a large office desk. There was a seat and a control consul and a TV screen to look at the images. Except there were no images.

They introduced Hartman to McDonald, the engineer. Young, male, long blonde hair tied back in a pony-tail, a business suit over a dark navy tee shirt with some kind of mathematical symbols all over the front of it and the statement that "lasers do it discretely", none of which made much sense to Hartman,

"So I suppose you found this problem before the show opened this morning?"

"No Sir, I was still back at the hotel having breakfast. I wasn't due here until late afternoon to supervise taking the instruments apart and packing them for shipping. The problem was discovered by the sales group when they went to fire the instrument up at about 8.15. There was no image on the screen and the signal default was showing. After a while they called me. So I got here about 9.15."

"So then what happened?"

"I started to check the instrument out and in about 20 minutes I established that the detector was missing. It's not the sort of fault anyone was expecting of course, so I had checked out a few other possible causes for loss of signal first."

"Was anything else missing?"

"Well the salespeople told me the machine was in the set-up mode when they arrived. That was odd, there was no need for a new set-up. We did all that last Friday when we fired up the instruments before the show. During the set-up alignment procedure, that's all automatic under computer control, there is a small metal screen that comes across to protect the sensitive detector and expose the alignment detector. I found that the screen was also gone."

"What does that mean?"

"I've no idea why the screen should be missing, it's relatively unimportant technology. Maybe whoever took the detector wanted to save time and not have to make-up a new screen for it. You see there is a larger, conventional detector in the same detector assembly. We use the screen and the conventional detector for initial alignment. The whole thing is automatic of course, controlled by the computer, and the screen protects the inner sensitive detector from being damaged by overload during alignment."

"How long would it take someone to get the detector out of the machine?"

"If they knew what they were doing, maybe five, ten minutes".

"And how long does the automatic alignment take?"

"About 30 seconds."

"Do we know if they did an alignment?"

"No."

Hartman turned to Walther,
"So in about 5 minutes someone could have taken the detector. And they could have done that anytime between the close of the exhibition and this morning."

"That's right, but the exhibition floor has to be clear of exhibitors and visitors by 6pm. In the morning only exhibitors are admitted before 9am, they can come in from 8am."

As an attempt at security, Hartman was not impressed,
"Sure, but whoever did it could have been in the John at 6pm last evening, come out and done the job say between midnight and five past, gone back into the John for the night and walked out of here this morning. And it's so small they could have carried it out in their closed hand or in a pocket without anyone knowing a thing. And sure enough, nobody saw anything unusual."

"Right."

Hartman continued relentlessly on with his analysis, using Walther as a non-participating listener as he developed his own ideas on the situation,
"So, what we know is that whoever took the detector must have known what they were doing and for some reason they also took this protective screen. That it must have been taken at the outside between 5pm yesterday and 8am

to-day. I presume all your competitors and perhaps a lot of other people would know how to open your machine."

"Right."

"Marvellous, we're in great shape, I hope you had it insured. If you did, you can be damn sure your insurers will want some serious security next year. The military are going to love you Parker-Wotton guys."

Goddam crazy scientists, they weren't safe to be out on their own. By now it could be anywhere in the entire fucking world. Fucking Iranians could have this by now. Another damn impossible problem, dropped into his lap. Shit, more fucking shit. What the fuck was he supposed to do about this? What the fuck could anyone do about it now? His stomach started to hurt again as he stood outside the Convention Center, he lit a cigarette and waited for a cab.

It was 2pm when Hartman got back to his office. He sat himself down, his large bulk sprawling in his standard government issue chair, in front of his office computer terminal, sipping his hot coffee with the low-cal sweetener and the artificial creamer, punching in the names he had gathered this morning from the Parker-Wotton booth and searched for records on them under the search command of "recent & updates". This way he would access some initial defining file information and additions made within the last 3 months and, if he needed, he could immediately access the complete file. Nothing of any real interest, odd facts about some aspects of their personal lives, army records and so forth in the initial summary section. Walther was gay, McDonald had been arrested for drugs possession when he was a student but no up-dates had been made recently for either of them apart from listing some routine visits to government laboratories for business. Then he looked up the more senior personnel. Parker, apart from some general identifying and publicly available information, the file was barred to him, no access available at his level, in fact no access except from the very top. Next he tried Ryan, Jim, and found nothing there except some summary details of his career, when he entered the States, then recent visits to military sites and government research locations and the very high security clearance he held. It was useless and in a final idle gesture of futility he scrolled the screen through the various "Ryan" listings. He took his finger off the keyboard and got up, the screen stopped scrolling and showed a search file for Ryan, Tom, initiated in an FBI office in California. He dismissed it along with the endless stream of other information all of which was of no interest to him, after all, there were lots of Ryan's.

He was walking over to dump his plastic cup in the waste bin specially allocated for plastic cups, when he remembered that the computer was displaying recent information only. He crumpled the empty plastic cup in his fist and threw it into the waste bin. The stomach pain started gnawing at him again, it was all symbolic of the contradictions of life he decided, he needed the coffee and the coffee attacked his stomach. The Tom Ryan search file had to have started or had something updated within the last 3 months and it was in the active category. Someone else in the FBI was looking for information on this Tom Ryan. Almost certainly, he thought, it was purely coincidental, but just maybe, just maybe, there was a connection. He looked down at his coffee cup now in the mess of all the other discarded used cups, turned away and went back to the computer terminal and pulled up the complete listing of facts gathered under the recently activated Tom Ryan search file.

# Chapter 20

The price Bansan had agreed with Yamatasan, President of the Hamanoshi Corporation, was $2.5M to be paid to Bansan's overseas account. This was much better than Bansan had expected. He had been surprised that Yamatasan had immediately expressed great interest in getting hold of the detector. This had been re-assuring to Bansan in setting-up the deal, it seemed clear to him that the information in the documents had been understated if anything. In Bansan's experience, that was unusual for the Americans, who normally oversold everything. Yamatasan did not even inquire how this extraordinary opportunity had come about, that was a business matter for Bansan and his colleagues, he simply seized it as a very fortunate solution to a grave business problem.

For Yamatasan, the technical advances in the Midon detector, it's acquisition by the giant Parker-Wotton Corporation and the consequential effects in the marketplace were of such dire importance that all the Japanese manufacturers had been approached by him. It was the correct Japanese way to proceed, and besides, the Ministry would not look favourably on a single company deal which would leave the other Japanese manufacturers in ruins and excluded from the international market. So the unit was being purchased cooperatively by the Hamanoshi Corporation and the other four Japanese manufacturers of Electron Microscopes. They would share the cost and share the technology and so stay in the business against this threat from the US Parker-Wotton Corporation. The competition between each of the five Japanese companies was less important than that they should all be able to benefit from the big international market.

Even with everyone dedicatedly working sixteen-hour days, it took the research lab at Hamanoshi four days of intense work to modify one of their instruments to accept the detector. It took one more day before they admitted they could get no signal from it apart from the standard detector incorporated as an outer ring around what was supposed to be the tiny ultra-sensitive detector. They weren't sure why. The special consultant from Kyoto University suggested that there must be some reason why there were two detectors on the one chip. Why was the standard detector there surrounding the ultra-sensitive detector? Perhaps it was for alignment reasons? If so, could they have exposed the ultra-sensitive detector to too much power? No, respectfully, they didn't think so. They had been very careful. They had checked their notes and procedures yet again. Without any viable explanation, they were left with just confusion and mutual embarrassment.

Perhaps the detector did not work at all; perhaps the unit

at the exhibition had been a fake? It would not be the first time a new instrument had been shown, apparently working, but in reality still full of unsolved problems. The Japanese knew, just like everyone else in the business, how intense was the pressure exerted on all exhibiting companies to launch new products at the Pittsburgh Conference. There was often a big time difference between what was apparently available at the show and the actual reality of a deliverable product. Sometimes the reality of what was shown and promised was not available for a long, long time after the show, sometimes the claims made for new instruments never became real. But, having something "new" at the show was essential to marketing and for publicity. Everyone wanted something new and better.

A week after they had first obtained the detector, the Director of Research at the Hamanoshi Corporation consulted the Research Directors in the four other instrument companies and they collectively made the decision that they would proceed to take the detector apart, then they might at least get some information about what the Americans were up to. It would help their own development program. Not as much as they had hoped, but they would learn more about the American technology than otherwise. There was nothing more they could do. Fortunately, representatives of all five Japanese manufacturers had been working on the project together in the Hamanoshi lab, otherwise distrust could have developed between them. It was a stressful time, but with renewed efforts, they would catch up with and overtake the Americans. That was always the way. And now that all five companies agreed they would continue their cooperation on this project, they felt stronger. Faced with the threat from the USA, they would pool their financial resources and technical know-how. A concerted effort would be made to outpace the Americans. This was the Japanese way. They all agreed this was a good outcome.

Yamatasan invited Bansan to have dinner with him in one of the finer Geisha houses in Tokyo. Bansan was honoured by the invitation and a little surprised and also a little concerned. The dinner would be excellent, the traditional Geisha dinner service a delight and the Geishas would be charming and skilled in the arts of love. But he was a little uneasy and felt sure there had to be some specific reason for this invitation. The reason possibly related to their recent business transaction.

When the evening was almost finished and the two beautiful and naked Geishas had bathed them and were now carefully massaging oils into their tired old bodies, Yamatasan spoke,
"Bansan, we were a little surprised with the detector you provided, the research group could not get it to function. Possibly it had never functioned and the Americans were over-optimistically making claims they could not fulfil. But

that does not correspond with the information we have from our sources at the Conference. We believe the device was almost certainly working at the exhibition. An alternative possibility is that it was supplied to you already and knowingly damaged. For us it is a disappointment to some extent, but still the whole project has been very useful. I am telling you this as a respected friend of many years, so that you may be careful if you do business again with your source."

It had been done with great politeness, great courtesy, but Bansan realized it represented a very serious loss of face for him with Yamatasan. He offered to re-negotiate the terms, but this was politely declined. Yamatasan said they still thought the exercise worthwhile and he was sure there would be long-term benefits. The information was being supplied to Bansan as a friend of long standing.

Bansan considered what he should do. He knew who had supplied the detector, Dr Jim Ryan, Marketing Vice President of the Parker-Wotton Corporation, California. A photograph taken with a miniature camera in the New Orleans bar had provided a sure identification. The question he now considered was, why. Why had this deal been set up for him? How was Kara connected to this and what was an appropriate response from him? The loss of standing with Yamatasan was not a small matter. He thought that Yamatasan too could have been embarrassed by the outcome and that was extremely serious. Perhaps there was still an opportunity here to rescue something? But time had slipped by, it was now ten days since he had completed the deal in New Orleans and he needed to resolve this quickly now. Quick decisions were not his way, not the Japanese way, yet he felt committed to taking some action in this matter. In the light of Yamatasan's comments, it was unacceptable now to leave the situation like this. Something decisive was required,

"Yamatasan, I am most appreciative of the courtesy you have shown me. I will act decisively to correct any shortcomings with our supplier and I can only ask to be given the opportunity to be of service to you in the future, both personally and in business."

Yamatasan replied that he was sure Bansan could be of service to him in the future. This formality was of some slight re-assurance to Bansan. He would think of a suitable large gift for Yamatasan, of course, but right now he was filled with embarrassment and could feel the quiet rage, that burned like fire under his skin, even as the Geisha continued to rub in her soothing oils.

# Chapter 21

"Amanda, my dear, you remember Tom, Tom Ryan my old student?" and then Maitland immediately added, "But of course, we are all getting older these days!"

Amanda was a striking woman, tall thin, with a good facial bone structure, very straight back, straight black hair tied back with a severe black bow, sharp intelligent eyes, dressed in a warm and robust horse riding style heavy coat, jodhpurs and boots, all suitable for being outdoors on this fresh morning in March. As she dismissively shook hands with Tom Ryan, she didn't look too pleased to be included in the "getting older" remark.

It was a Saturday morning, March 25 and they were standing at a temporarily fenced off area in the middle of a large field. The field was just one of many in a rambling old country estate of rich parkland, between the towns of Bray and Enniskerry in Co. Wicklow. The big Georgian House could not be seen from here. Access to the field was through one of the functional farm entrances, off a small twisting road and marked by a neatly painted sign in black letters saying "Pony Camp" and complete with an arrow. They were at a Pony Camp for the sons and daughters of the riding classes, mainly the daughters. The rest of the field was seemingly randomly covered in horseboxes towed by four-wheel drives. Those who could not afford the only rational method of pulling horseboxes around the countryside and across fields, had large old cars and older horseboxes. The surface of the field was becoming tracked and churned up with such heavyweight traffic. Reluctant horses and ponies were being coaxed in and out of the horseboxes, children were being screamed at by excitable mothers. Impossibly tiny children were recklessly and seemingly randomly, galloping their long suffering ponies all over the place. Altogether a picture of total bedlam. Within the fenced area were arranged a number of jumps of various designs and some sense of order prevailed within the enclosure.

The two Maitland girls were in the fenced area, riding their ponies over the jumps under the sharply observant eye of Amanda. When they finished and the watching collection of parents, mainly mothers, had applauded the girls, Amanda made some comments on how they rode each fence. The main advice from Amanda to her daughters seemed to be the requirement for "more leg" when riding at the fences. Perhaps it was this odd sounding expression, but Ryan started to wonder about how it would be between Amanda and Maitland. Such a brittle, no nonsense woman, another marriage of opposites. Could this woman ever relax, become sensual, he wondered? How would she be when she came, did she ever come at all?

Amanda, after a brief glance in the direction of Ryan and Maitland, continued her lecture to the girls as Maitland and Tom excused themselves. They started to walk across the field, heading towards a wide, tree lined riding track which cut and climbed slowly through the parkland, it's edges defined on each side by stands of old deciduous trees. Maitland went into one of his general discussions as they passed through the parents, children, horses and ponies. The business of the IRA was not a topic for discussion in these surroundings. Their serious, private discussion would have to wait until they reached the seclusion of the Old Long Gallop making it's way through the trees. Maitland continued to make conversation, effortlessly it seemed, in his discursive, unworldly tone,

"One has to be supportive. It's a strange thing marriage, it gets you into all sorts of odd situations and children are even worse. You really have little or no control over their interests and passions. Of course, marrying a woman who has had an interest in horses since her own childhood, doesn't help. This is definitely not my cup of tea. Oscar Wilde was right when he classified the hunting fraternity as the unspeakable in pursuit of the uneatable. These days they may not all be occupied entirely by hunting the uneatable, but they themselves are still very largely to be numbered in the unspeakable category."

Tom laughed as Maitland continued to describe his predicament,

"You know I have formed the opinion that a lot of horses truly despise human kind. They look down on us, regard us as inferior with our absurd requirements of them, our irrational ways of behaving. One of our own horses certainly looks at one with complete contempt, the long suffering, condescending expression in her eyes puts one immediately in ones place."

Tom laughed again,
"I doubt if Amanda shares your views!"

Maitland replied in his serious, almost detached manner,
"No indeed, her approach is entirely pragmatic. We keep the horses, they in return perform as we require, or else."

"Yes, but I would say that Amanda's viewpoint is shared by most of the people here to-day."

Maitland made a resigned sigh to Tom's comment and then went on with his discourse,
"Ah yes, I am certainly in a minority, I do realise that. It is nevertheless quite interesting to see the Irish Horse Protestants at play, so to speak, and this kind of thing is still very largely in the hands of the Protestants. Some of the local peasantry who have been successful in commerce, the law or whatever, have joined the horsy set, but they are still at one remove. On some of the minor and more obscure committees in Trinity, one also still sees the Anglo-Irish Protestant "ethos" in full vigour. This is a fascinating

glimpse to the past, gives me a feeling of closeness to how things were in Trinity and the country in general, particularly from the Anglo-Irish point of view. Of course one sees the horse keeping class in England also, but there the social situation is different. Here it is overloaded with not just social, but with so-called ethnic tones as well. These days the more acceptable word "ethos" tends to be preferred."

They walked on, nearing the seclusion of the trees and Maitland continued his analysis,

"But the horsey class in both countries share an extraordinary view of life really. A human life lived and measured through the prowess of a horse. As specimens of the human animal, most of these people would simply not rate at all. They have never been fit enough, competent or energetic enough to compete in a sport while relying entirely on their own bodies and athletic performance. Their achievement and sense of achievement is totally dependent on the performance of their horse. The other aspect which doesn't bear thinking about in the context of a healthy puritanical Protestant mind, is it's extraordinary appeal to young girls. But as I say, these are not matters I feel comfortable raising with Amanda or indeed the girls. It would be entirely pointless anyway. So, like the majority of fathers, I soldier on as best I can. But that's not a predicament you share, you and Hazel had no children."

"No and under the circumstances I have to say that I am glad about that."

There was a period of silence as they now walked on beneath the old trees, just coming into leaf. The luscious smell of the long grass covering the gently rolling country-side all coming freshly alive this early Spring morning in myriad shades of green, effortlessly thrusting forth from the bountiful earth. Maitland now changed tone, no longer the bemused academic, whimsically observing the world, and started to discuss the purpose of their meeting on that beautiful morning,

"So Tom, it's good to see you again. You are still alive obviously and I'm very relieved to see that. How did you get back into the country?"

"I took a chance and contacted a guy called Terry McIntyre. He was with me in the old days, when the old IRA had us running around the hills and mountains not far from here. On our absurd and totally useless training exercises. He has a problem with the bottle these days, but he seemed my best chance of getting back into the country without attracting attention. We go back a long way. It's strange how the bonds formed through shared experience when you are young seem to last. He runs a trawler now and picked me up in a small port in the north of France. The trawler, I may tell you, is a thoroughly unpleasant method of travel not at all enhanced by the combined stench of rotting fish and diesel. But I'm here, and hopefully McIn-tyre will keep his mouth shut!"

"What is the position about the funds, I presume from your cryptic telephone call that you are in a position to produce the necessary amount?"

"Yes, it's a long story, but you could say my brother did manage to find the funds. They are now in a bank account in Switzerland and I have the letter of authorization on the account."

"Excellent, excellent, that all sounds highly promising. Fol-lowing your phone call, I set up a meeting for you with a sub-group of four appointed by the Army Council who have agreed to give you a hearing. I just need to confirm it to them, but you can take it that it is all arranged."

"What sort of reception do you think I'll get?"

"Well, the positive aspect is that you have come back to face the music. That helps put you on the right footing as a start. Your friend O'Sullivan has of course, been very active in pointing the finger at you, all the confirmation he needed was the fact that you had disappeared. He wanted to have you sentenced in Abstentia, but there have been some other matters pre-occupying the Council in the interim and this has helped you. A decision on O'Sullivan's proposal has been deferred. Despite the cease-fire continuing to hold, the pressures within the organization are building up. The lack of progress in the negotiations is irritating the military wing and the cease-fire is in jeopardy."

"Surely the cease-fire can't break down, not this soon into the negotiations?"

They turned around and started walking back through the long straight gallop, back towards the general area of hubbub, and Maitland replied,
"The feeling is that the British and indeed everyone else, are all delighted with the peace, but no one seems in any hurry to move on. The militants are now saying they always claimed nothing would come out of the present negotiations and want to get back into the driving seat. Naturally I have been closely involved with the whole process, since they use me to read the political and strategic situation from the British side and advise. So your little local problem has not received the attention it might otherwise have, which is fortunate really. I did get the idea floated through the Council that possibly under the circumstances, even an innocent man might have thought it wise to disappear for a while in the hope that the money might be found. Also and less successfully, that in the present delicate circumstances, a local hit was not what they need. But of course, the matter of internal discipline is regarded as removed from the general conduct of the war. In any event,

that's how matters stand right now. All things considered, it seems to give you a reasonable chance of success."

They parted, Maitland putting a hand on Tom's shoulder as they shook hands and wishing him good luck, before returning to Amanda and his daughters.

Tom Ryan walked back toward his car, only to find it blocked by a much larger and older car attached to an old style heavy horsebox complete with a mother and young teenage daughter trying to encourage a reluctant and very large horse to get back into the box. He was irritated at the delay and by the thoughtlessness of the pair in blocking him in and was about to tell them so. Instead he thought of the contrast in their situations and their respective problems and what brought each of them to this place on this Saturday in Spring. For the mother and daughter it was all about the horse, getting it in and out of horseboxes and how it performed in competition. They had created their problem. He had created his. For him it was about coping with the IRA and staying alive. He started to laugh out loud at the ludicrous comparison of their two problems. The mother heard him in the midst of her struggles with the horse and looked at him like she wished to kill him. In any event, he thought, life went on, it was only a question of how you lived it, planning and worrying about the future were to an extent ridiculous, it seemed we only exerted limited control over what happened, life was teaching him that. But for now at least, he was alive and he should make the best of it. He stretched out his arms, looked up at the bright blue sky and the lush green colours of Spring. The horsewoman gave him another un-amused look and impatiently told her daughter to pay attention to the problem of the horse. Tom Ryan leaned back against the side of his car, looked at the blue sky and thought about making love to Kara.

# Chapter 22

It was the Wednesday night following his meeting with Maitland at the Pony Camp, when Tom Ryan drove into the carpark of the pub in the Dublin Mountains. "The Green Lantern" was perched on the side of a hill, a narrow twisting country road passing by it's front walls, two gaps in the wall giving access to the loose stone surface of the carpark. From the carpark there was a clear view out over the Irish Sea. The place had a rough feel about it. Very much Traditional Irish Country Pub. It was popular with tourists in the Summer and with bikers all year round. He was sure it was effectively owned by the IRA, one of the pubs they had bought. Trading in pubs was one way of laundering funds, as he well knew. This one they had kept as a very convenient meeting place, the location remote and isolated, yet within easy reach of Dublin. It was 10.00pm precisely as he pulled into the rough uneven surface of the car parking area beside the pub buildings.

A group of musicians was in one corner, playing another lilting old time ballad for a smallish mid-week crowd. Two of the customers standing at the bar looked like they had other things on their mind, their eyes watchfully sweeping the bar-room and the entrance doors. They spotted him as soon as he walked in, probably had him monitored from arriving in the car park. Once he had entered the car park, there was no going back. This was it. One way or the other, his future would be decided.

There was a very large guy with a pint of Guinness standing casually up against the closed door that led to the stairs and the upstairs room. White shirt, open at the neck, exposing his big frame and beer belly, all partially covered by a dark brown tweed jacket. He levered himself off the door with one shoulder as Tom came over, said nothing, just let him by. The serious eyes belying the easygoing appearance and not looking at Ryan as he passed. As he had levered his bulk forward, the outline of the shoulder holster could just be seen under the jacket.

Ryan opened the ill-fitting old wooden door to be immediately faced with a solid steel door set into a steel frame. He pulled back the heavy steel door and looked up a flight of dimly lit, steep wooden stairs, only wide enough for one person. At the top of the stairs his eyes met those of another guy, small, dressed entirely in black and openly cradling an automatic pistol. He beckoned Tom up with a quick uplift of his head, showing no expression of any sort of emotion as his eyes darted over Tom. As Ryan reached the top of the stairs and stood on the small landing, the guy with the automatic told him to wait. They weren't ready for him yet. Still holding the weapon, he ran his free hand over the outline of Tom Ryan's body, checking him for weapons.

The broken sound of muffled voices came through the door to the upstairs room, masked by sounds of the traditional music coming through from the floor below.

The room door opened and O'Sullivan came out, "Nice to see you again, Tom. It's your turn now."

He went in. Four of them sitting facing him on the other side of a big old wooden table, a single uncovered light bulb hanging down from the smoke discoloured ceiling above the table. Some papers in front of each of them. A starkly empty wooden chair for him opposite them. He sat down. Three young guys he didn't know. The fourth an older guy he recognized from '69 and Derry. Kelly, Pat Kelly, yes, that was who it was. He still looked fit, but the fiery, passionate, determined young man he remembered had now aged to mature years. Ryan looked into Kelly's eyes and could see the dark shadows of the troubled years, the difficult decisions had taken their toll. Kelly spoke,

"Well Tom, we meet again after all these years. I remember you coming up in '69. They were difficult times. We had nothing, nothing at all. You know it gave us great heart, Tom, when you and a few others came. Too few to do anything except give us heart. But that isn't forgotten, Tom, not by me and the others who were there at the time."

Tom Ryan nodded his appreciation, but wasn't sure what to say next, so he just said,

"Thank you."

Kelly went on, his voice showing a little weariness now,
"Personally I have never believed that people change. They
may make small changes to their lives, learn a trick or two,
change how they go about this or that. But basically, the
more I see, I don't believe that people change at all. Not
deep down, not for things that count. That I suppose is one
of the problems we have, but it is also an advantage, in
your case at least. You see, I can't figure out how a guy
like you could ever steal from the organization. It just
doesn't sit with me. You're getting on a bit now, Tom, even
older than I am! Perhaps too old for the rough and tumble
of the game as it is now played. We can come back to that,
but I for one would need to be convinced very hard that
you have turned rotten. O'Sullivan sees it his way, but then,
he wasn't in Derry in '69. That counts with me. Our comrades here weren't in Derry in '69 either of course, too
young. But you and the others who came had a choice. You
came, that makes the difference. Too many chose to do
nothing. Go on a march in Dublin maybe. Talk their
mouths off in pubs. But they didn't put themselves on the
line. So now Tom, let's hear your side of it."

Tom explained what happened on the night of the robbery,
as far as he knew it. Getting out to the drop point at
2.15am, finding nothing at all.

One of the younger men with a tight carpet of red hair sticking up like a shoe-brush from his head, the pale blue eyes jumping out at the world from his skull-like, parchment white, thin face, sharp Northern accent,
"Just how do you explain that?"

Ryan replied,
"I can't. I have no idea what happened, what the sequence of events could have been. The arrangements were perfectly straightforward. There seems no reason why they didn't make the drop."

The red haired guys response came in a stylised tone that was both questioning, mocking and sure of itself,
"So you have no explanation for what happened to the funds?"

"No."

"There is a theory about that you could have taken them. You were the one to go to the drop point, we only have your word that the funds weren't there."

"I wasn't the only one who knew about the arrangements. It is possible to argue, for the sake of argument only I am not accusing anyone, that let's say O'Sullivan went out there and picked up before I got there."

The younger guy continued, not at all impressed, his hard Northern accent matching his hard line,

"That would be stretching things a little too far, for my money at least. OK so let's say the funds disappeared and we have no idea how. Now you're here saying you can replace them. Just how did that come about? It all sounds very interesting, you'd better tell us the details, we need to be convinced."

Tom didn't want to go into more detail than he could, but he knew he had to say enough to convince them,
"My brother raised the money by selling an item to some Japanese businessmen in the States."

"It's a lot of money, why would your brother get involved, he has no connection to us that I know of?"

Tom began to wonder if they were playing nice guy, hard guy with him, if it had all been rehearsed,
"He wants me out of the organization."

"I see. You realise that an alternative view of all this is that you stole the money and are now giving it back to us."

"Why would I do that? It makes no sense."

"None of this makes sense. How are the funds to be given back to us, now that you say you have them?"

"I have the original letter of authorization on a Swiss bank account. As you will notice, the signature releasing the account to the bearer is that of a Japanese. That relates to what I told you about the deal my brother did."

He passed the letter across the table to them. The older one, Kelly, spoke again,
"Alright Tom, please wait outside and we'll call you back in a little while."

The guy standing outside the door was not surprised that Tom waited. Neither he nor Tom said anything. It was obvious that nothing should be said. There was no social dimension to his waiting with the guy who was cradling the automatic. He noticed the music coming from downstairs again. He had been oblivious to it while in the room. It only added to his edginess. It stopped, some applause and rowdy drunken shouts of encouragement and appreciation from the listeners. A break. Unclear conversation coming through the door. Then another tune started up. Jesus what were they deciding? He could be taken for a one-way ride now. Anything could happen, he was powerless, totally dependent on what happened behind the closed door in that gloomy room with no windows lit by its single glaring light bulb.

He heard the footsteps coming across the bare wooden floor and the door opened,
"Right."

One of the younger ones, he wondered was that a good or bad sign. He went back into the room and sat down again on the lone wooden chair on the near side of the table. Kelly looked at him, didn't say anything for a moment. The silence hung, was all-present in the room, Tom could no longer hear the band. He could smell and taste the old dried wood dust in the air along with the smell of damp mould oozing from the old building. Kelly spoke, his tone formal,

"By a majority decision, we have decided to make the following recommendation to the Army Council. That your return of the funds be accepted along with your explanation. That you be stood down from active service with immediate effect."

It took a moment for it to sink in to his stressed brain. His brain felt numb, but as clearly as he could, he said simply, "Thank you."

Kelly again, more casual now,
"Tom, this sub-group has often to make hard and brutal decisions. It's inevitable in an organization like this, with the difficulties we have with informers and renegades. But this war has been going on for so long now, that some of us are dying not from the risks of active service, but from old age. Despite the day to day problems of what we are engaged in, we have a structure and an operation which has

gone on for as long as many businesses. But we are not good at man management, so to speak. We have no early retirement plans, no way of even saying thanks to people like you who have given the best part of a life's service to the Cause. So I want to take this opportunity to acknowledge what you have done over the years. As you know, there is no way out of the IRA; you are just being stood down. You could be called upon in special circumstances at any time. But it seems to me appropriate that you be acknowledged now, despite the circumstances that brought us together to-night for this committee hearing."

"Thank you again."

He felt that this was not just a message for him; Kelly was trying to bring a bigger picture to the attention of the younger men, moderate their views and their actions perhaps.

"Good luck Tom."

He stood up and Kelly walked him to the door. The guy outside hardly moved his eyes, but he saw Kelly shake Tom's hand and then nod.

Down the stairs and out the stairway door. The outer wooden door was already swinging slightly open when he reached the bottom of the stairs, the big guy guarding the entrance to the stairs must have heard him coming and moved aside. O'Sullivan was sitting at the bar, a glass of orange in front of him. He nodded, gave a greasy smile as Tom passed. Out through the bar and out into the fresh air. The cold night air tasted like wine. In the mountain sky the stars twinkled their crisp message of hope. Dear God, dear God he was out, it was over.

His mind started to wonder what would have happened if they had not reached their majority decision in his favour, how close was the decision? What would they have done with him if they had decided against? Killed him, for sure. But how and when? Maybe he wasn't free after all, this could have been just a charade. Perhaps after all he had been tried and sentenced in Abstentia. That bastard O'Sullivan was still in the pub. But, Kelly seemed to be entirely sincere. Walking slowly across the rough, unlit car park at the back of the pub he prayed. When he turned the key in the ignition he was praying even harder.

# Chapter 23

O'Sullivan was pleased to have been given the task by the IRA. It was an important mission. On the Dublin to Zurich flight, he looked like a slightly impoverished businessman, wrinkled suit and over-sized brief case, flying economy. In the almost empty brief case he now had the bank letter of authorization that Tom Ryan had supplied to the IRA and his false Irish passport in the name of Blake.

When O'Sullivan presented the documents at the bank in Zurich and asked for cash, the soberly dressed young executive requested him to come back the following day, "I'm sure you understand, Mr. Blake, that our Documentation Verification Department must check authenticity for a transaction like this, there is only this letter to substantiate our handing over the funds in this account to you. Two of my colleagues must satisfy themselves that all is in order and sign their names to the authorization."

O'Sullivan didn't like the arrogant condescending tone, enunciated in a superior, super-perfect English, by the tall, thin, formally dressed Swiss with the black rimmed glasses. But he decided he'd better agree,
"Yeah, right, I'll be back to-morrow."

"And how would you like payment, Sir?"

"Large denomination US$ bills will be fine."

"Of course, Mr. Blake. Shall we say 9.30am to-morrow if that's convenient for you?"

He returned the next day at 9.30am and they paid him in US$ cash, large denomination notes, total $495,000 after charges. The 1% handling fees he hadn't expected, but he only needed $370,000 as the payment for the arms deal. Trust a Swiss bank to charge you for paying out your own money. He took a taxi directly from the bank to the airport and booked himself on the next flight to Paris. He just had hand luggage with him and he went to the gate and waited for an hour and a half before boarding the flight. By the time he arrived in Paris, he had arranged the cash in two large envelopes, one for Gerhard von Bruening that he marked with the letter "B".

Paris in the late Spring of 1995, Tuesday, April 4. Full of visiting tourists and lovers strolling along the Seine or through the parks and squares. Tourists busy with their plans to see this, photograph that. Lovers lost in their closed world of two. The light green of the young leaves filling the trees with reborn life and promise.

The information he had been given on von Bruening said he was ex- East German Security. When von Bruening had been a good Communist, he was just Bruening. But now there was democracy and the capitalist world, so he had re-introduced the more aristocratic version of his name. Not that the name change did anything for his manners or ideas of civilization. His objectives in life remained the same, his view of how society fundamentally operated, that too, remained the same. He was still an unscrupulous thug right down to the expensive socks in his expensive shoes. He had managed to survive the political change because of the information he held on a wide variety of people, east and west. He was now ideally placed to engage in the arms trade, high level blackmail, and the various other dubious ventures he had running.

O'Sullivan was to meet von Bruening at a speciality fish restaurant, near the Madeleine. The restaurant was fronted to the street by a long expanse of lightly coloured, plate glass window, edged in chrome and with a chrome edged glass entrance door. Inside the restaurant the light airy atmosphere had been maintained in the modern chrome furnishings and glass topped tables. The green plants hanging from pots on the walls giving a natural, healthy feel to the whole place. It was a nice restaurant, the food was good and it was anonymous. The location, von Bruening knew, would leave both of them clear of each other after the funds were passed over. He had originally found it some years previously with a girlfriend he had brought to Paris, it was a place well suited to his business purposes and one he used every now and then.

They had arranged to eat early, that way the restaurant would not be crowded and their quiet table in the corner, away from the window wall, allowed them to conduct business. von Bruening was a large, bull-like man. Broad shoulders, powerful body, dark brown hair brushed straight back over his large head, slow movements, a threatening physical presence. Hard and rough. To O'Sullivan, he looked like he should have come from Bavaria, a big prosperous Bavarian farmer perhaps. But of course, he wasn't from Bavaria. von Bruening had the boisterous exuberance about him of one who had been enjoying the fruits of his ample cash income for a number of years now. He felt secure, everything was under his control and going his way. Life was good.

"So, what wines will you take, I'm having the Graves, it's a very dry Graves and should be ideal with the oysters I am having to start. What do you want?"

"I don't drink."

von Bruening was having trouble with the accent, "Could you say that again?"

With exaggerated slowness and clarity and with increased volume, O'Sullivan re-stated his position, "I don't drink alcohol."

von Bruening looked at him quizzically over his copy of the extensive and excellent wine list. This looked like it was

going to be a difficult interaction. He ordered water for
O'Sullivan and reconsidered his original intention to order
a bottle of Chateau d'Yquem for the end of the meal, as
was his custom on these occasions. He had been looking
forward to a pleasing termination of the meal by indulging
in the luxury of the outlandishly expensive and very sweet
desert wine. The wine had come to symbolize the sweetness
of his deals successfully completed in hard cash. Instead he
decided he would settle for a good Cognac for himself when
the time came.

For von Bruening, Ireland was simply the location of one
of his many customer groups. He had little interest in the
detailed reasons why they were buying arms to pursue their
long-standing local terrorist activities. Fighting the British
of course, well that was understandable. Beyond that, he
had just enough knowledge and understanding to keep him
out of trouble, make sure he didn't get caught between the
two sides and that he knew who he was dealing with.

These days, for von Bruening, there wasn't time enough to
keep track of all the details of his many and varied customers. But the Irish situation looked like it would go on
indefinitely and that was good for business. The cease-fire
hadn't seemed to interfere significantly with business.
Once-off deals were always more dangerous, more expensive to set-up, repeat business was what he liked, just like
most businesses. The Irish seemed to have an enormous

capacity for arms of most types and he knew they dealt with a number of other suppliers apart from him. World arms prices were now very competitive, the workings of the capitalist market economy and the need for hard currency in the former Communist countries was being reflected by prices in the arms business. But at least it was one of the few commodities they had that anyone wanted. There was an ample supply of all kinds of arms on the market. Still, the demand was also good once you had the right contacts. That's what the business was all about. The right contacts, and he had them for both the supply and demand side. Business was still good, life was good. You just had to be hard and pushy and in von Bruening's world there was no place for the weak. Never had been.

Over dinner, what little stilted conversation there was had awkwardly revolved around Paris and the things to see and von Bruening was irritated to find himself leaning forward in an attempt to understand the almost incomprehensible accent of his dinner companion. Everything that was said was kept very non-specific, no life stories were going to be exchanged here, but von Bruening regarded himself as a sharp judge of people and enjoyed observing their little weaknesses, yet he couldn't find a way into this miserable little man. There was nothing there to relate to. No suggestion of some perverse desire or pleasure and he didn't look like he had ever been directly involved with violence. Von

Bruening looked across at O'Sullivan again. No, he certainly wasn't on the hard side of the business. Wouldn't have the stomach for it. Physically insignificant. An organizer. An apparatchik, the type von Bruening knew intimately. Their small creeping minds, devious and dangerous. But they fell apart soon enough with the right treatment, just a little brutality or even just the threat of it expressed in clear language.

von Bruening ordered his Cognac and looked across at O'Sullivan,

"So, you like this Pope?"

"What Pope?"

"There is only one. The one in Rome."

"Why would I know anything about him?"

"I presume you are Catholic, so you should know about him."

"Fuck the Pope, I'm a Marxist."

There was silence. von Bruening finished his Cognac. O'Sullivan was fidgeting with his glass of water. von Bruening was not a man easily astonished, but when O'Sullivan asked him to sign a receipt, he was totally amazed. This was definitely not normal, this guy must be new to the job.

Just didn't understand the realities, probably an accountant by profession, small potatoes. No problem, he ignored the pen offered by O'Sullivan, took out his own expensive pen and scrawled an illegible signature for $370,000. Fuck him, just what did he think that meant? Was he really thinking they would end up in court discussing the validity of von Bruening's signature? The last guy the Irish had sent had been easy going and they had gone on to a nightclub after the deal. Keen to see the naughty side of Paris to which von Bruening was an excellent guide. Anyway, what the fuck was he doing with another envelope in his case? Was he going to make another payout to-night? von Bruening put his envelope into his own briefcase. No need to count it. They still hadn't had delivery, the ball was in his court and the IRA wouldn't have any interest in screwing him. It was time to leave this miserable specimen of humanity. He beckoned the waitress for the bill. In his clear, deep, rough voice, he said to O'Sullivan,

"You will excuse me now, we have completed our business. I must be on my way as you say. I hope to do business again in the future. The delivery will be made in the agreed way within the next two weeks. Your people take over in Hamburg."

"Right, I'm not concerned with the delivery side. If we're doing business again, I see no reason why you can't come over to Ireland and save me this journey."

"Unfortunately that would not be possible, I make a point of never visiting customers premises."

As he paid the bill in cash, von Bruening reflected that he was at least fortunate that this fool had not addressed him by name. He made a mental note to himself that in the next deal set-up with the IRA, he would make it clear about who they sent. People like this idiot could put you in jeopardy. That was not part of von Bruening's way of doing business.

It was nearly 8.00pm when they left the restaurant and each went their separate ways. Both men had hotels within easy walking distance. The two Japanese men who had also had dinner in the restaurant, bowed to each other as they too parted outside the restaurant before going their separate ways. Two Japanese businessmen observing the correct familiar ritual, showing respect to each other by their repeated quick low bows, incongruous in Western eyes, like a couple of mad chickens. They too had paid the restaurant in cash, but without waiting for the bill. The large payment they left on the table delighted the waitress. Japanese, she thought, must have just arrived and obviously didn't understand the currency yet, they'd paid her an excessive amount in Swiss Francs.

O'Sullivan had been booked into a relatively small, inexpensive hotel, out of the way in a narrow side street. A place unlikely to be used by many Irish. Certainly no big tour groups, not enough rooms. He stepped into the small elevator to take him to his room on the fourth floor. Just before the door closed, he was surprised to find a Japanese also stepping smartly in. Small guy, but very stocky. O'Sullivan thought that a little odd. Not the kind of place you'd expect to find a Japanese businessman. Even he knew they attached great importance to the standard of hotel they stayed at, believed it reflected on their status. A strange people the Japanese, but it takes all sorts.

When the elevator arrived on the fourth floor, the Japanese stepped out and immediately went back down to the ground floor, this time using the stairway beside the elevator and carrying O'Sullivan's briefcase. O'Sullivan was propped up in a sitting position on the floor of the elevator, dead, with the door jammed slightly open by his left foot. Often the simplest and surest way to do something is very boldly, very directly, very quickly. And with total surprise. The Yakuza noted the odd coincidence of it being the fourth floor. The number four was unlucky, it represented death. But then, the ignorant Geyshing would not have known that.

von Bruening walked leisurely back to his spacious plush room in the international five star hotel on the Avenue de L'Opera. He was glad to be out in the evening air, stretching his legs and loosening his large body on the short walk back. It had been an irritating evening and that stupid, petty Irishman was not at all interesting as a dinner companion. He wondered what was going on with the IRA that they sent someone like that, perhaps there were problems. Perhaps he needed to think about that and re-assess his position in terms of his dealings with them. He had survived and prospered by learning to take small signs very seriously, often it was all he'd had to go on in his precarious and dangerous career. The wrong people used for the wrong job could be dangerous and expose him to unnecessary risk. In any event, it was done for now, he would worry about the implications of possible IRA incompetence tomorrow. He had the funds, the deal would go through and now there was the delightful prospect of Birgitte back in his comfortable hotel room.

His little blonde from Dresden. She was a delight, the ideas she had! There was no doubt about it in von Bruening's mind, he definitely preferred German girls for sex. You could be sure they had carefully studied the manuals, watched the videos, took it all as a serious study and become properly expert. He had no need for the emotional overtones, no talk about orgasms being like death or that sort of Latin nonsense, it was just an experience, a desirable and necessary part of life's pleasures. The essential ingredients were simple, youthful female attractiveness combined with agility and good technique. Like in so many of life's practicalities, he thought, the Germans had it mastered. Like German built cars, they looked good and functioned reliably. Sex was the same, no need for any emotional nonsense, an entirely practical matter, that's the way he liked it and he liked it at least once a day.

When he entered the room, she was lying naked like a lightly tanned curvaceous sexy blonde butterfly in the enormous bed. A bottle of champagne open and in an ice bucket beside her, an appetizing cold buffet laid out on a room service table. Beautiful. Perfect. This was life. Birgitte smiled invitingly to him as he came into the room and she ran her hands down her naked, tanned and suggestively wriggling body.

He had hardly closed the door when there was a sharp business-like knock. Damn, maybe room service again, no doubt the staff had forgotten something she ordered. He opened the door and just had time to see a Japanese businessman. The surprise and irritation had hardly registered when his nose was hit by a hard, fast upward moving all powerful palm and pushed up into his brain. He didn't feel the two hands make the chopping blow on each side of his neck to make sure he was dying.

As von Brüening's body was pushed aside and back into the room, falling heavily to the floor, Birgitte started to scream. But by then the Japanese was already in the room and had closed the door. As she tried to pull the cover over her, he was at the bed and hit her a crushing blow with the side of his hand across the front of her young, delicate throat. The result was to produce a choking near silence. Then he strangled her, his hands grasping the sheet under her neck to provide purchase for his crossed arms. The hardened sides of his two hands pressed in a vice like clamp against each side of her beautiful neck. She was dead in twenty seconds; he maintained the pressure for a further ten seconds.

As he quietly left the hotel, no one noticed anything. A Japanese man leaving this five star hotel with a briefcase. Nothing unusual, Paris was full of them and the large Japanese tour groups. They all had plenty of money to spend. One of the pretty young receptionists in the hotel lobby smiled at him as he passed. The Yakuza nodded formally, didn't smile.

*Fax message to Bansan, Paris, Tuesday, April 4, 1995:*
*We have the honour to report that your total expenditure has been recovered, less minor costs. All contacts with financial matters terminated through three exits. No residual interests or problems are apparent. Will arrange banking of proceeds to your account to-morrow in accordance with your instructions. We propose returning to Tokyo earliest available flight unless we can have the distinction of further service to you.*

Bansan grunted nasally with satisfaction as he read the handwritten Japanese script written on the Paris hotel notepaper. The one page message had come through to his private fax at home as he breakfasted before the start of the new day. Whatever the other parties to this deal had wanted to achieve, the funds were central. Removal of the funds was sure to provide repercussions for all those involved, including, he thought, Dr. Jim Ryan. No further action was needed; revenge had been taken, swiftly, effectively and with an elegant style. His plan had been implemented in an entirely satisfactory way and the whole process appealed to his Japanese sense of how things should be done in such cases of treachery, a devastating strike against the enemy when least expected. He wondered who were the three who had been killed by the Yakuza, but then, that was just a detail. Bansan was confident that the ripples from this stone he had cast into the pond of life would spread out and reach all those who had crossed him. Then he thought of Kara and was filled with a powerful sexual desire. He thought it strange how this action had taken place in Paris, where he had first been with her. He wanted her now.

# Chapter 24

Life for Tom Ryan was getting back to normal little by little with each day that passed. He had resumed his job after his three months leave and was busy catching up and re-establishing himself in the Western Regional Development Authority. Everyone said how well and fit he looked and that the leave of absence had done him good. His boss, Duggan, was understanding and delighted to have him back. The receptionist smiled at him and blushed each morning when he told her how beautiful she was. The relationship with Kara was not yet back to it's happy norm, but he assumed they just needed some time after the stress and separation of the past months. Then came the news of O'Sullivan's death. All over the TV, Radio and newspapers with headlines of the type "Irishman murdered in Paris — Robbery Motive". Of course it should not have anything to do with him, he was out now, but an uncomfortable chill gripped him, it was far too close to home for comfort. Perhaps he was becoming paranoid, he thought. He considered going to see Maitland again, but it seemed pointless, he couldn't keep running back to him every time something happened, anyway, whatever Maitland could do had been done and his aloofness from the brutal reality on the ground made him of even more limited use with this.

On Friday morning, April 7, Seymour was digesting the latest information available from the media and his police contacts on his recently deceased client, O'Sullivan, aka Blake. The Irish news media had said nothing specifically about von Bruening, just mentioning that two German visitors had also been killed in their five-star hotel on the same evening. The von Bruening factor he had picked up from his own investigations.

Whatever had happened to O'Sullivan, Seymour hoped this at least would be an end to it as far as he was concerned and he could get back to his more routine matrimonial cases, security problems and the lucrative business of providing bodyguards for visiting movie stars and rock stars. There had been no recent visit from Fitzpatrick or any of the others from the Special Branch. So far so good, maybe next week would be the start of his new life, a more normal life where he could get on with managing his business and only know about the IRA through the newspapers and only knowing enough about them to stay out of their way.

Madden buzzed him from the outer office,
"Mr. Seymour, I'm sorry to disturb you but there's a Mr. Ryan here to see you, a Mr. Tom Ryan. He doesn't have an appointment but he says it's important. Are you available to see him or should I make an appointment for him?"

Seymour's breath caught for a moment, then he said,

"I see, you'd better send him in."

Tom Ryan was ushered in, Seymour stood up and shook him by the hand and exchanged the usual pleasantries. The picture he had obtained of Ryan had not shown the scar on the left side of his face. He remembered the file information about Ryan being shot when he was a youngster on active service with the old IRA. The reality of Ryan's presence was more powerful and dynamic than he had expected from the old picture. True he looked a lot more world weary, but the old spark was still there, the kind of spark and single mindedness that leads people into foolish or romantic actions. He asked Ryan to sit down,

"My usual question to someone entering this office is to ask how they selected my firm. In your case I imagine I already know, but you had better explain it to me in any case."

"I don't want to consume your time with long-winded accounts of what you probably already know. Let's start from the fact that I recently came back to Ireland on McIntryre's trawler. I've known him a long time and this was a personal favour to me. In the course of the journey he mentioned that if I had any more difficulty with my problem, I should seek you out. He seemed to believe that you knew more about what was going on than anyone else."

"I suppose the old scoundrel was drunk when he suggested you look me up?"

"It's hard to know in the case of McIntyre whether he's drunk or not, the word probably can't be applied to him in the normal sense. Anyway, he didn't go into detail, just told me you were a separate operation with nothing to do with the organization, at least directly, but that you had become involved by accident and that he believed you knew a lot more than he did. And that you were reliable."

"Well, that was very decent of him. I presume your arrival here might have something to do with Mr. O'Sullivan's little accident in Paris?"

"Yes, I thought I'd settled matters with the organization. Maybe I'm becoming paranoid; I don't know why O'Sullivan was in Paris or why he was killed. Even though I am supposed to be officially stood down, it leaves me feeling very uncomfortable."

Seymour thought that Tom Ryan was certainly not the only one getting paranoid around here. Maybe he should set up a sub-section of his office to provide an IRA counselling service. There seemed to be no end to it,
"But, just for the record, you weren't in Paris last week?"

"No."

"And your trip to the US was successful, I presume, in coming up with the funds to replace those missing since the robbery Maguire staged?"

"I don't know how much you know about that, but the short answer is yes."

"Then I'm sure O'Sullivan's death can have no bearing on matters for you. Who knows what happened, but an arms dealer was killed on that same evening, maybe the deal went wrong, maybe they both got ripped off, who knows. But since you weren't involved and you have sorted matters out with the organization, it seems clear that all this has nothing to do with you."

"That would seem entirely reasonable, but this whole situation has no reason attached to it from what I've seen. Until recently, O'Sullivan wanted me killed. Now he's dead, murdered in Paris. I simply don't feel that this is going to pass me by."

"I'll try to keep an eye on anything that comes out in the way of further information, but all you can do is put this to one side and maybe just be very careful how you go. I could offer you a bodyguard, but that would only attract more attention to you and that's not what you need right now. Just watch out for anything that seems unusual and take defensive action. Of course, I realize that if you do become a target again, they are likely to make a very serious attempt to kill you. But as you say, you may be just becoming paranoid. Why should you be a target, there's no reason, you're not involved anymore?"

When Ryan left the office, Seymour went to the window overlooking the street below. No one outside that he could see. The visit from Tom Ryan was pulling him back into a problem that he wanted to be done with. He went out to where Madden was typing into the computer, he could still hear Ryan's footsteps going down the stairs. He spoke in a low voice to Madden, his irritation overcome by concern at what was happening,

"You'd better go after him and check that there is no sign of a tail on him and get the registration number of the car he's driving if you can and then come back."

Walking back into his office he decided the sign outside the building should read "IRA Counselling and Assistance Centre — All Welcome".

# Chapter 25

"For the love of Jesus, what the fuck is going on here?".
Tempers were getting heated at the full meeting of the
Army Council. They were gathered around the old wooden
table upstairs in the "Green Lantern" pub on Saturday
night, April 8. The complexities of the debate about the
continuing cease-fire and the report on the negotiations by
the politicos had stressed everyone out. The militants were
angry now, sidelined as the process was now being handled
entirely by the political section. Their tempers were given
vent by the lack of progress being reported from the negotiations. Standing down a military operation was not a simple matter. Now there was the prospect of unconditional
disarmament being required by the British and that was
just bloody well unacceptable.

The next item on the agenda was a straight military problem and it was the last straw in setting fire to the meeting.
It exposed the military section to criticism from the politicos, gave them leverage in the debate.

"Sweet Jesus, we couldn't even make a simple cash hand-
over in Paris without our man getting killed and the fucking
money being ripped off. And the fucking arms dealer and
his fucking whore are also fucking dead. Would you like to
explain that Kelly? How does that fit in with our strategy?"

Kelly was an old hand at this now. Patience was all-important in any type of committee work, this was no exception. The more troublesome the problem, the more important it was to stay cool. Give them time to say their piece and argue it out between themselves and they would see the way forward all by themselves. He had learnt a long time ago that jumping in with his own previously and carefully thought out solution was not the way to get agreement. A word here and there to guide them a little, but let them believe they had thought it through and decided it for themselves. That was always his policy, but this time he was worried, the climate that had developed at the meeting, the bruised egos and feeling of helplessness all meant he wasn't entirely sure he could bring them around,

"First we should hear from Intelligence. Let's all try to keep calm."

The entire group sitting around the old wooden table, turned to another of the older men.

"All our sources say this is not British Intelligence or any other covert body who might have an interest in us. There is no way any known or suspect informer could have set this up, not according to the best information we have. The fact that von Bruening is also dead indicates that we weren't ripped off by his group."

"You can't be certain of that."

"No, but that's the best indication we have from subsequent contacts. His people, and he only had two close associates, are sure of that. Of course, we can't know all the factors with a bastard like that. He was up to all sorts of games, including blackmailing politicians. A number of people could have taken him out for a variety of reasons from his past. But then you have to ask, why take out O'Sullivan as well? And after they had left their meeting — if they had been taken out together, then you could have said he was just in the wrong place at the wrong time. But he was targeted too. It doesn't make sense. Not unless you base it all on opportunistic robbery and that doesn't sit well with the idea of someone taking revenge on von Bruening. And a double opportunistic robbery is not on."

Another of the younger men,
"What about other Intelligence services, the Germans for example?"

"Not likely, again for the same reasons. If they wanted von Bruening they would have no interest in taking O'Sullivan out."

The younger one came back again with the same line of argument,
"What about a collaborative operation between the British and the Germans or even the French?"

"Possible, but not likely. We don't think the British could have a lead on O'Sullivan, as that theory would seem to require. If it had been someone at this table, yes, but he just didn't rate that kind of priority with them. Anyway, the method of the killings is not typical of the British. If the British had done it themselves it's likely they would have used a silenced gun for a killing at close quarters. O'Sullivan was killed by hand, by an expert. Anyway, the whole operation was a damn sight too slick for the British."

"What about the possibility of a new specialist field group formed within British Intelligence, that could have provided a new range of operational techniques?"

"If anything like that had happened we would have known about it from our own source to the British Establishment. Any structural changes would have been forwarded to him. It's just that type of structural information that makes him important, among other things. Anyway, O'Sullivan is a most unlikely target, hardly worth the exposure if they had some new structures in place."

"So, let's get this clear, having considered all possibilities, you're telling us that our Intelligence group cannot find a lead?"

"Apart from the obvious."

"Which is?"

"Tom Ryan is the only common factor to the previous problem with these same funds and with O'Sullivan. Again we find ourselves in precisely the same situation as after the Meat Plant Robbery in Castleglen. The funds are missing and everyone actively connected to the operation is dead."

"Do you have any definite information that could link Tom Ryan into this, why would he want to do it?"

"The answer is no, we don't have anything definite, but Tom Ryan is the common thread."

They all turned to look at Kelly. This was awkward for him, the mood of the whole meeting had gone away from him, he was appalled by what now was emerging and confronting him but tried to remain detached, business-like, "I still don't believe it, it couldn't be him. He had no reason. It makes no sense."

The first younger member came straight back at him, "Why not? You came to us with a majority recommendation after your Discipline Group hearing. There must have been some doubt even then. Now we have another entire debacle on our hands. How much more of this are we going to put up with? Remember, you sent O'Sullivan to his death."

"I've sent a lot of men to their death directly and indirectly, just like everyone else around this table, it's part of the operational risk in war. I've learnt to live with it. But I do try to make sure we don't needlessly take out one of our own, particularly when I'm sure all he has done is serve the Cause."

Apart from the noise coming up from the bar below, there was silence in the room. The younger man stared across the table at Kelly, and said in a clear, slow hard voice,
"I want a vote on this, this repeat performance, with Ryan again at the centre, this is one performance too many for me."

# Chapter 26

In New Orleans, the temperature and the humidity were increasing side by side, settling in for the long, slow-moving, sweating heat of a Southern summer. It had become kind of a hobby for Gus Hartman, to look into the FBI computer and see what turned up under "Ryan". By now the investigation into the robbery at the Conference Center had been taken out of his hands and from what he could learn, had gone precisely nowhere, just as he expected. He had a feeling about this though, he was now convinced that Jim Ryan was involved and that Tom Ryan was involved. Tom Ryan's departure from the States to Frankfurt and his return were all known to him. And now his departure again from the States, to Frankfurt again just a couple of days after the robbery at the Pittsburgh Conference. A search back through the VISA section of the US Embassy in Dublin gave him information about Tom Ryan being convicted in the Fifties for his part in the border raid. Hartman didn't add this to the still active running file. But now he had a theory — that Jim Ryan had somehow stolen the detector and that Tom Ryan and the IRA were involved. Much though he liked his theory, he decided there was no point in taking this to his smooth talking, desk jockey of a young boss. God only knew what the politics of digging into this would be right now. Wedged between the political and financial power of the Parker-Wotton Corporation and the delicate state of the IRA cease-fire in Ireland, there were a million reasons why it would not be progressed without any firm evidence. Plus it was no longer any of his business anyway. And he had no proof at all, absolutely nothing on which to go saying that Dr. Jim Ryan, Senior Vice President of Marketing at Parker-Wotton had stolen the device. At best he would be told to go away and forget it. At worst he would have another note added to his personnel file questioning his professional judgment. He could do without that.

Hartman put a call into the California office and asked to speak with the agent who had opened the trace file on Tom Ryan. The agent told him the computer file was opened on a favour for favour basis for a detective in Ireland. They owed him for something from way back. No it wasn't the Irish police force, this was private. Hartman told him he was going to Ireland on vacation in a couple of weeks and would look him up and say hello, it might be a useful contact. The agent gave him the contact name and business address, John Seymour with offices in Dublin, Ireland.

He had thought of taking his wife for the trip. But the complications and explanations that he would have to come up with for her as to why he, Gus Hartman, composed of generations of undiluted solid Pennsylvanian German genetic stock, would be taking a trip to Ireland would be difficult to say the least. That he could do without. So he told her he would be away on FBI business for a week. She just looked blankly at him and said nothing.

He told himself he wanted to win one, a big one, a really big one, just one, before he quit the FBI. He booked a bargain week Irish package holiday for himself with a hotel in Dublin included. The flight into Dublin touched down at dawn on Saturday, April 8 and he had an appointment to see Seymour on Monday morning.

Hartman's first words on entering Seymour's office were accompanied by his heavy, wheezy breathing,
"Jesus H Christ, those stairs, how do you live with that?"

The sheer bulk of Hartman seemed to occupy an enormously disproportionate share of the volume available in the space of the office. Large areas of white wall disappeared behind him, his whole dark rounded bulging form stood pulsating with the effort of getting up the four floors, exuding the sheer physicality of it all through his considerable presence. Seymour stood up and extended his hand,
"Good morning Mr. Hartman, why don't you have a seat."

His hand disappeared into Hartman's grasp,
"Yeah I could do with a seat. I'm still recovering from the diarrhoea I had all day Saturday after that damn transatlantic flight. How the hell they expect you to sit all night in

those tight seats I have no idea. It's not human. And last night I couldn't sleep at all, this trip is gonna' kill me."

"How did you select us Mr. Hartman?"

"Got your name from a colleague of mine in California."

Hartman flashed his FBI identity and passed a business card across the desk. Seymour tried to show no reaction, his mind now racing. Following the news that O'Sullivan had been killed in Paris, he really thought he was out of this whole mess. Seymour had decided that Tom Ryan was just paranoid, even if understandably so. There had still been no further visit from Fitzpatrick. He had been sure it would all go away. But now there was this, the start of a new week and Gus Hartman of the FBI sitting in his office. As a matter of routine, he pressed the photo sequence button on his desk while Hartman continued,
"Yeah, I work out of New Orleans as you would pronounce it, or as the locals like to call it Nawlins. I have your name in connection with a file opened for you in the California office and in which I have an interest."

"Is that so."

Hartman had caught his breath by now,
"Yeah".
He paused and then asked,

"So, tell me what you know about Tom Ryan and his brother, Dr. Jim Ryan."

"Not a lot. But why has the FBI come to me, why not go straight to our security forces, the Special Branch — they would be your opposite number over here as I'm sure you must know?"

"Well there are a couple of reasons. One being that this is potentially sensitive as we see it, so we want a little discreet help here on the ground. And, as usual, we don't want our friends in the CIA in on it or getting to know about our interest in all this. You'll understand that I'm sure."

"To the best of my knowledge, Mr. Tom Ryan is a perfectly respectable business executive."

"So why were you interested in him?"

"A client of mine who is associated with Ryan wanted to find him and thought he had gone to the USA. It all came to nothing and I've closed the file. My client is no longer interested."

"Well I guess this Tom Ryan must be a fascinating guy, since now you have me as another client who is interested in him."

Hartman took out a photograph and passed it across the desk to Seymour,

"See this, this is what I'm trying to find and I think our Tom Ryan may well have it or did have it in his possession."

Seymour looked down at the enlarged black and white photograph; it showed what looked like a big computer chip with two concentric rectangles on top of it. A six-inch scale shown in the photo lying beside the chip indicated that the chip was about two inches long and about half an inch across. At one end it was printed with the name Midon and at the other there was a code number. Hartman leaned forward, the chair creaking under him, and pointed a large index finger at the photograph,

"You see that number, that's a US Military Code Number, a MIL number on the chip. That means that this gizmo is kinda' important. We're a little touchy about who gets their hands on it. I have to tell you that would include your business executive Mr. Tom Ryan. "

Seymour remembered that his late client had been killed with the arms dealer von Bruening and silently swore to himself as Hartman continued in his southern drawl,
"Now this here ain't the identical part, this is one the military have as you will no doubt appreciate from the MIL number. But one that was stolen in New Orleans recently is much like it."

"Mr. Hartman, this seems like the proverbial problem of the needle in the haystack, except on an even smaller scale."

"Yeah, but this here is a real expensive and important needle and we want our little needle back."

"You have some kind of plan?"

"I sure as hell do, I want to know every damn thing this guy Tom Ryan has in his home, from toothpick to who he sleeps with and what he dreams of. I want for the two of us to go pay his place a nice long visit and see just what he's got there. He's got this thing someplace, that's for sure."

"You have some evidence of that, Mr. Hartman?"

"Enough evidence for me to be here looking for Ryan and our missing little toy. Did you know that Tom Ryan was in the IRA and served a prison sentence?"

"Well I have to tell you that would not make him entirely unique in this country, nor would it necessarily mean anything about his present activities. As I already said to you, I know he is a respectable business executive with a government agency."

"Oh yeah? And all that don't necessarily mean a damn thing, as I'm sure you know. But as a professional, I guess

you have no problem helping me and the US Government
in this exercise, particularly since the FBI seems to have
done you a favour or two already?"

Seymour thought he had plenty of problems apart from
helping the FBI, but that he had no choice but to stay in to
maintain some measure of control of the escalating
situation,
"No, indeed, Mr. Hartman. I provide a professional service
to any legitimate client. Maybe I should clarify my fee basis
for you first so that there is no misunderstanding. I presume
the FBI will be the billed entity?"

On Tuesday they went through Tom Ryan's place in
Castleglen. Found nothing. Hartman decided it was too
clean, but took a spare set of keys he found, noted a few
addresses and telephone numbers including those for Kara
and for Ryan's parents. On Wednesday they went through
Kara's apartment, using Tom Ryan's set of keys to get in
and using her fax machine to make copies of letters in
Japanese. They had found nothing of significance. Hartman
said it would be too slow to use the FBI's own language
facilities in the USA to translate the letters. He asked
Seymour to arrange for a rush service, and agreed to pay
whatever additional costs were involved. The Japanese letters were in turn faxed by Seymour to a private translation
service in the United States to provide some distance from
Kara's own business language service.

The translations came back early the next morning. Most of the material was of no interest, all they found out was that she had a Japanese lover, Bansan. And that she and he had been jointly involved with some kind of business deal recently. Hartman next wanted to break into Ryan's parent's house, but Seymour explained this was going to be more difficult since they were likely to be at home all day. Hartman was getting impatient, and for his next move he told Seymour he wanted to steal Ryan's car and take it apart. And if he didn't find anything there, he wanted to break into his office and the Western Regional Development Authority.

Seymour's hope, that Hartman would eventually run out of steam or get re-called back to the States for something more important than this little computer chip, was not looking good.

On Thursday morning Seymour drove them back again to Castleglen so that Hartman could check out Ryan's car in the carpark of the Western Regional Development Authority. They stopped for lunch at McDonalds. Hartman had a large fries and a Big Mac with a vanilla milk shake followed by a large coffee which he used to wash down two large tablets he had taken from his pocket, all of which seemed to leave him thoroughly rejuvenated. During this interlude to re-fuel Hartman, Seymour had a paper cup of tea and contemplated this next action. By now he was becoming increasingly sure Hartman was a maniac, a wild card, driven by some private obsession. He thought that perhaps it might be useful for the FBI to have the services of obsessive personnel, but Hartman was becoming increasingly dangerous to him. He was almost certain that Hartman must be on a private mission of some sort, without the official backing of the FBI. At most, he thought, this was some unofficial operation by the FBI or a section within the FBI. Hartman seemed to be operating alone, the whole thing had an odd feeling about it, there seemed to be no on-going contact between Hartman and the FBI.

They had got in and out of the two apartments alright and Seymour was reasonably sure that the break-ins would not be so obvious as to be noticed unless someone was checking very carefully. He had infuriated Hartman by his cautiousness, but as he explained, he, Seymour, had to live with any fallout. His attempts to convince Hartman to wait until nightfall before attempting to check out Tom Ryan's car had proved futile. Hartman, he decided, would have to be the one to take the car, he wasn't going to risk it himself.

Hartman had no problem with this,
"Ain't no problem, like I always says, you want to take something, do it in broad daylight and right up in front of everyone, that way, no one pays any attention to you at all. You try steal something looking all shifty at night, you got everyone's attention."

"OK Gus, the arrangements stand, I'll see you back at the garage in Dublin as agreed. To-night we'll take the car apart and later abandon it so it looks like it might have been stolen in the usual way. As I said before, you get caught, I've never seen you in my life."

"Hey, I got the key to this guy's car, piece of cake. We're takin' delivery."

Seymour dropped Hartman off near the Western Regional Development Authority site, turned his car and headed back up the Dublin road. As he was passing the Castleglen Meats Plant, he saw Tom Ryan as a passenger in another car heading into Castleglen. Presumably, Seymour decided, he was travelling with a colleague back to the office after some morning meeting. Hartman would need to be quick. He consoled himself with the prospect that everything would close down to-morrow for the Easter weekend and maybe he could send Hartman off on some kind of sightseeing tour and have a peaceful weekend. He was getting tired of being trapped into this whole mess.

# Chapter 27

Kara had noticed how Tom had begun to relax a little since he had told her he was out of active service for the IRA. The stress had gradually started to leave him, he was becoming more fun again even if during last weekend he had seemed distant. But he was reading his books, talking with her, going to the theatre and the movies together, telling her he wanted to get away on a holiday together with her. And he was starting to talk about their future together.

That was not so easy for her. She didn't know what she wanted anymore. She had told him her parents were getting old and feeble in Tokyo, she felt she should help them, go and live there with them in their last few years. He had just escaped from the IRA, he wanted her, to live with her, wanted life with her. How could she go to back to Japan? Surely what they had was so special that they should hold on to it, tightly, all the more special because they had found each other late in life and with the loving fire of teenagers?

She didn't tell him about Bansan. How he had been faxing her and phoning her. Saying he was retiring this year and had bought an entire small island close to the mainland of Japan. The battle she had with herself about this. Did she not want to establish life again in Japan, where all the customs were familiar? Rather than face spending the rest of her life here, in the land where she was an outsider, part of the small separated and ever changing Japanese community. Perhaps it was time for her to go back to Japan.

It was Thursday evening, April 13 and she was waiting for Tom to arrive at her apartment to spend the Easter Holiday weekend together. The setting evening sun was casting a red glow across the bay, over to Howth and lighting the headland with a pink hue. He wasn't due for another hour but she already had the Japanese meal ready for them. All his favourite Sushi and the other things he liked, delivered by her friend from the local Japanese restaurant. The two women had talked and joked. It was good to speak freely in Japanese to her friend. They had an easy understanding and liking for each other, both being about the same age, both living in this distant country. Exchanging gossip about the various Japanese they both knew, mainly businessmen posted overseas without their wives. Who was having affairs, laughing together at the latest vulgar jokes they had heard from the Japanese men of their acquaintance, comparing the latest misunderstandings and funny things that happened between the two cultures.

Now she was alone, waiting for Tom and thinking her thoughts. Standing at the big windows looking out at the evening and the gently changing light across the bay. She remembered how it had been when they first met. How he

seemed so different, the fire behind the eyes, the sponta-
neity, his easy laughter, how he liked to make her laugh.
How quickly she had known she wanted him. How he had
given her a joy in life, made her feel young again, made her
feel like a woman, wanting to please him, make him happy,
be special for him. There had been no one like him, she
had never felt like this, not since she was young and first
fell in love with her husband. That was all so long ago. She
had not expected, never planned, to fall in love again.

Suddenly she thought someone had come into the apartment. She was surprised, she wasn't expecting Tom yet, not
this early. But she was sure someone had come in. She went
to the door. Closed, no one there. She looked around,
everything was normal, just as before. Part of her was certain no one could have come in, another part insisting that
there was someone there, in her apartment, had just come
through the door. She could feel the presence of someone.
She felt her body go cold and she became very frightened.

The awful feeling wouldn't leave her alone. She had never
before felt disturbed in any way in this beautiful, secure
apartment. But the eerie feeling that someone was there
wouldn't let her go, a whole part of her was sure someone
had come in. It was ridiculous, she knew. No one was there.
The view from the window was just as before, gentle and
peaceful in the delicate changing evening light. But the feeling wouldn't go away and she couldn't shake off the cold

and the fear. For some strange reason, part of the poem "Losing You" came into her mind,

*I stand, stand limp*
*Unable to think or do*
*There is a void within me*
*And in this void my mind hunts for you*

# Chapter 28

Funerals. As a policeman, John Fitzpatrick went to more than his share of these. Part of the job, he mused. But this one was different in all sorts of ways. The Irish seemed to have a special gift for funerals, probably just as well. He had attended a couple in England, not the same at all, dreadful affairs. To-day another part of the Castleglen affair would be closed off. The three in the Meat Plant robbery, then O'Sullivan. But there was no IRA symbolism here, no gloves, no flag, not at the funeral of Tom Ryan.

Fitzpatrick was standing at the back of the big Church on the south side of Dublin, looking carefully at the gathering for this Funeral Mass. He was here as a discreet observer from the Intelligence Section of the Anti-Terrorist Force, a sort of human camera. Suit, shirt and tie, shoes polished, looking smart enough to be inconspicuous in the crowd, an inconspicuous camera monitoring the scene. A good turn-out though, lots of respectable people from the Western Regional Development Agency. But they weren't the interesting ones. He was here to check on those who might have some special connection to this. Not the family, not the job, the IRA was his interest. An IRA funeral on the Wednesday after Easter, an unsettling feeling even for Fitzpatrick, given the significance of Easter and the 1916

Easter Rising in the mythology of the IRA. The shared symbolism of Death and Resurrection for both the IRA and the Christian Church. And the delicate relationship all this had with the existence, the very birth, of the State he served.

Not that he had much hope of coming up with anything new, but it all helped the Intelligence Service piece together what was going on in the country. All the more important though at the moment, with the cease-fire still intact.

His eyes travelled over the attendance gathered in the cavernous, grey formality of the large neo-Gothic Church, first looking at the principal mourners, the family. The father, not looking at all well, stooped and broken. Used to be a big wheel at one time in the Department of Finance. The mother, trying to bear up, stay strong, keep from crying, not succeeding. The younger brother, Jim, back from the USA, not showing much emotion, trying to hold everything and everyone together.

The routine check Fitzpatrick had asked the FBI to run on Jim Ryan was clear. Almost too clear, no contact with any Irish group at all. Just that odd cross-reference in the FBI computer to an inquiry about Tom Ryan being in California. All the FBI had tracked and logged into their computers was his visit to the USA before Christmas and a subsequent visit. Tom Ryan had certainly covered his tracks well. It hardly mattered now, but he wondered why and who had triggered the initial inquiry with the FBI. It was certainly odd, if there was enough time and resources it should be followed up and cross-checked to see what it revealed, but he thought that wasn't likely now, there were more immediate problems to be attended to with the IRA.

Fitzpatrick looked across at Jim's attractive wife, Ellen and the two very American looking kids. Strange how the son, Kevin, looked remarkably like that old faded newspaper picture of the young Tom Ryan on the files. Tall, handsome, sturdy and tanned. A walking advertisement for California. Odd how that old IRA bastard Kelly, had seemed to make a point of talking with Kevin the previous night when the remains were brought to the Church. Probably of no significance, all sorts of odd people talked to each other at funerals. The daughter, Jean, beautiful and blonde, just like the mother.

Hazel, the ex-wife, looking totally shattered and distraught, standing beside Jim, his arm around her. She looked like she was coming apart. From there his eyes moved to the Japanese woman, Kara, the girlfriend. Off to one side. Isolated, removed, no proper place for her here. The lover had no position at a family occasion like this, there could be no place for her, no matter how they had loved. The complexities of modern life, not encompassed within the formalities of this funeral service. She looked old, her face sad and strained, her skin hued with grey green and crumpled, but no tears. Left with a few letters and photographs. The person he had cared most about before he died.

Fitzpatrick had learnt about Tom Ryan's private life from the search of Ryan's apartment by the Security Service. The love letters from Kara. The photographs of them together. Older photographs of him with Hazel, getting married, other family occasions. And the love letter to Kara written by Tom and never sent. Did he die thinking of her or did the immediacy of the car going off the road occupy his mind in those last moments? This job juxta-positioned the practicalities of people's lives and their grand passions and feelings. Not for the first time he had thought how absurd peoples most vital feelings seemed when read by strangers, indeed, how absurd sexual love seemed to the outsider, the observer, either as the physical act or as expressed in words. Both could so easily be seen as ridiculous. But that touched on the problem, was life defined by its practical achievements and failures or was it in reality defined by feelings? He looked over at Kara again. Perhaps in the end, feelings are all that mattered. We are defined, exist only, in terms of our feelings and dreams. Attempts to produce practical changes seemed largely incidental, reality for the individual was experienced through these most ephemeral of things, feelings and dreams.

The priests voice echoed and floated around the church,

seeming only to emphasize the lost loneliness of death. Violent death. That was what always brought him to these funerals. The ceremony of death. There was no doubt about it, the Irish were good at it. The ceremony to console the living, but what about the one who is dead, how is the sense of conscious being interrupted in sudden, violent death, is it like switching out a light, what happens to all the feelings, the personality, the desires? He thought that if you took a purely materialist, non-spiritual view and death was like switching off a light, then for the dead, the world itself must cease to exist. There is then simply nothing in the absence of conscious being. Perhaps that's why the ceremony of death is so important for the living, to assure themselves that they are not dead, that life goes on. That the world continues to exist. At least until it's their turn. Then their world will end, which for them is, of course, the only world. There can be no more world then, all of creation is wiped out by the death of the individual as conscious being ceases.

Who knows? Damn all you can do about it anyway. Life, death, you have no choice in the absolute nature of both events. We don't know where we come from or where we are going. Death awaits us all, and we face it's awful reality or try to hide from it, without any understanding. Probably one of the great achievements of the human mind, that it can continue to function, provide a feeling of normality in the face of such an incomprehensible and inevitable, out-rageous event. If the human race had any sense at all, we should all be stark raving mad contemplating the prospect of death. No wonder, he thought, we need funeral ceremonies.

Fitzpatrick resumed his observation of the attendance, the still living. Maitland and his wife, both looking elegant, dig-nified. He wondered what this tall, upper class Englishman, distinguished scholar of Anglo-Irish Literature and pillar of respectable society, would think if he knew he was standing in a church with members of the IRA? If he was told that his former student, now deceased, was up to his neck in it?

The organist started to play a Bach fugue. High piercing notes then the deep rumbling notes that flooded the church with wrenching emotion, reverberating in Fitzpatrick's chest cavity. Who the hell do they think they are burying, some kind of saint? Fitzpatrick wondered if Ryan had asked for this music before his death. Hardly, he probably wasn't expecting death, had made no arrangements. Per-haps if you are in the IRA you should plan your funeral well in advance. Perhaps we all should. His mind started to wander again, could you ask the questions, "How does Tom Ryan feel now?", "Where is Tom Ryan now?". What meaning did such questions have? What answers did they have? He decided that these damn funerals were getting to him and wondered how the hell the undertakers could

stand it. Confronted with it every day. Continuously
reminded of the appalling incomprehensible prospect
awaiting them.

Fitzpatrick moved his gaze again, to Duggan, the Regional
Head of the Western Development Authority. He was easily accounted for, simply the boss here to say goodbye to
his co-worker, a member of his staff. Beside Duggan was
The Chief Executive of the National Development Authority. Putting in the necessary appearance on the tragic
death of a valued mid-ranking executive, observing the formalities. Except, of course, that the Chief Executive knew
perfectly well that this was no ordinary funeral.

Then the others in whom he was more interested. Pat Kelly,
from Derry. Very interesting indeed, long-standing senior
member of the Army Council. Terry McIntyre from Galway. The Security Service had never got anything on McIntyre and his trawler, but they had raided him a couple of
times. You couldn't keep raiding him and finding nothing,
no matter how suspicious you were. For sure he was deep
in it, but you could never catch him. As slippery as the fish
in that trawler of his.

The Development Authority had clamped down on the
enquiry and stopped the results going public. After the
initial forensic examination of the car had found the
remains of the explosive device on what was left of the

brake master cylinder, Forensics quickly concluded it was a new type of device, electronically controlled to be temperature and time dependent, it would only detonate on a long run, half an hour after the engine had reached it's normal temperature. New improved technology. Much neater than blowing-up the whole car and possibly taking out innocent civilians. An arranged accident at a spot on a country road one Thursday evening. It would have been even neater if the bastards had got the amount of explosive right. The Church promised the resurrection of the body, the IRA certainly weren't assisting in that notion, what the forensics team had scraped up had gone into a series of bags and in the end it was hair colour and blood group that was left to identify him. Anyway, there was nothing to be done about it, no one was ever going to be caught and brought to trial for this murder.

He wondered if Ryan's killing could be connected to O'Sullivan's murder in Paris? Both from the same region in Ireland, Castleglen, and that region had gone mad in recent times. That crazy robbery and the mayhem it released. No IRA funeral for O'Sullivan either, he too was undercover. Described publicly as a Civil Servant, a dedicated and caring Social Worker, tragically robbed and murdered while on a short holiday break in Paris. Only the Intelligence Forces all over Europe had noted the connection with the murder that same evening of von Bruening, arms dealer and blackmailer. The Germans were far too concerned about the possible political consequences of von Bruening's untimely death to worry too much about any other aspects. Of course there was also the death of the pretty young girl from Dresden, but then, no one was seriously interested in her.

Tom Ryan's old time connections to the IRA had been easily turned up as an immediate consequence of the investigation of the car accident. His being taken out with a bomb was not the sort of publicity the Development Authority needed, for this was surely all part of the IRA. The Authority had plenty of influence and if you are bringing in important overseas business operations to the country, your crisp clean business image is vital. So this was put down as an unfortunate car accident, maybe he was speeding and took the corner too fast? A mistake anyone could make driving these narrow twisting country roads and hurrying to Dublin on a Thursday night before a holiday weekend. Sure, sure, but it didn't make any difference anyway. The cops weren't ever going to nail anyone for the murder of Tom Ryan. So they were kept out of it. It was a purely Intelligence matter now.

All the same, Fitzpatrick thought, the whole thing had a very peculiar feel to it. Even this low key IRA funeral. The bastards must have done it themselves, taken out one of their own. An internal matter, and yet McIntyre and Kelly had shown up. Just old friends from the past? Kelly at least knew for sure, he must have been in on the execution decision taken by the Army Council. And still he was here. McIntyre as well. He too probably knew what really happened. All very odd, he thought, maybe they were becoming even more like the Mafia, going to each others funerals having previously arranged the death. In any event, the IRA had one less active service member now. Not that that would stop anything. As far as Fitzpatrick was concerned, this cancer renewed itself through the generations.

He looked around and saw Seymour standing at the back of the Church. What the hell was he doing here, he'd tackle him outside and find out. After the Funeral Mass, as the crowds milled around while the coffin was loaded into the hearse and everyone there paid their respects and chatted to each other, Fitzpatrick caught up with Seymour who seemed about to leave,
"Seymour, what are you doing here?"

"Hello John, I'm paying my respects like everyone else."

"How did you know the late Mr. Tom Ryan?"

"I didn't, but he was a friend of Danny Maguire and I thought I should pay my respects."

"That was very nice of you, particularly since you are such a busy man these days. Odd mind you, you weren't at your friend Maguire's little funeral in the West, and yet you're here?"

"Maguire's was an IRA funeral, I don't go to such things. I sent some flowers and maybe I'll visit his grave someday."

There was a very slight pause before Fitzpatrick replied. He continued looking at Seymour, his face still smiling but the eyes now hard and thoughtful as he wondered if Seymour was playing his usual games with him and just how much Seymour knew about Ryan. He had never thought Seymour to be the kind of man to take time out for foolish things that were not important to him,

"Is that right now? I knew about the flowers, but I have this growing credibility problem with you these days. We must have a long talk soon, but you'll have to excuse me now, apart from yourself, there are a number of other interesting people here I have to say hello to, the kind of people I don't often get to meet on social occasions. It's been a fascinating funeral as these things go."

Fitzpatrick went off, heading in the direction of Kelly.

# Chapter 29

It was 12 noon in Seymour's office and Seymour had come straight back from the Church leaving most of the large congregation to go on to the graveyard after the Funeral Mass for Tom Ryan. He had told Madden to show the client he was expecting into his office and leave him there until he arrived. Seymour came into his office, taking off his overcoat and said,

"You did the right thing, keeping your head down. I know it wasn't easy for you, but you really shouldn't have risked going to the funeral. Being here is risky enough and you can't stay long."

"How did you see me at the funeral?"

"Maybe I was the only one who knew it was possible for you to be there. Anyway, you were hardly invisible in the parked rental car, a lot of people could have picked you out! It was a crazy thing to do. I want you taking no more risks, my neck is in this too!"

"It's not often you get the chance to see your own funeral in progress. It's dreadful what this has done to my family and Kara, but if I had contacted anyone over the weekend

I would have just set myself up as a target again and brought them all into danger."

"That's right. Remember that. I just wish I'd given you my home number, but I didn't think it would come to this."

Ryan had a five-day growth of beard that was coming out almost pure grey,
"Is there any immediate problem?"

Seymour looked out through the window and down into the street below,
"Not really, but you will have to go out through the back entrance with Madden, I see two gorillas waiting outside again in their car. Doubtless a visit from John Fitzpatrick of the Special Branch can be expected shortly."

"Who was in my car, who was buried to-day?"

"I seem to have developed the knack of loosing clients these days which is hardly encouraging for you right now. It seems to happen whenever they get too close to Tom Ryan, they end up dead. If it's any consolation to you, the latest would probably have died soon enough anyway, he struck me as a very unwell man. He was an FBI agent called Gus Hartman. I think he was on a private fishing trip for some reason. He'd got a bee in his bonnet about some computer chip or other which he says was stolen in the States. You wouldn't know anything about that of course. In his enthusiasm for the job he decided to steal your car to see if the chip was there. I helped him to some extent with that, but you could say his excessive American work ethic saved your life. He seemed a decent enough poor devil, in his own way."

"Christ. This whole thing is becoming more unreal."

"Certainly your funeral is doing nothing to detract from that! And you'd better stay dead, that way you're likely to stay alive longer!"

"What will happen about the FBI man?"

"Someone will no doubt miss him shortly. For a start he has a family in the States. He didn't have what you could call a happy family life from what he told me. But they and the FBI will no doubt notice his absence eventually. Then they will quickly track him to Ireland, maybe even to me here, but I cleaned out his hotel room of any references to me. I will tell them I never met him. There's nothing else I can do. He's dead. Referring them to the IRA as his murderer's is not going to help anyone."

"I thought when they got the funds replaced I would be safe and this whole thing would be over, I was supposed to be out of the organization, stood down from active service."

"Yeah, you told me. I thought when Danny Maguire died, that I was finished with my connections, but ever since it's got a damn sight worse."

"Do you think this is connected with whatever actually happened to the funds from Maguire's robbery?"

"No. Not directly anyway. Not to what really happened to the funds. I know what happened to the funds, it was always fairly obvious and it became even more so a couple of months ago. No this is not related, of that much I am at least sure. Right now I can only assume your friends have tied you in to O'Sullivan's death for some reason. I may be able to find out in due course from McIntyre. But you must stay dead. Tom Ryan is not a healthy identity for you or anyone near you anymore."

"I don't know how long I can stay dead. There's a woman I'm in love with, Kara, a Japanese woman, you must have seen her at the funeral?"

"Yes I know. I suppose now is as good a time for you to find out as any, but she intends to go back to Japan and shack up with a guy called Bansan or something."

"Jesus, how the hell can you know that, it can't be true?" But as he said it he could feel his stomach tighten.

"I don't wish to sound unsympathetic, we've all been

through it and you surely have enough other problems right now. But you must be clear minded, this is no time for stupid moves. What I've just told you is true. Hartman, with my assistance, broke into her apartment, that was after we broke into yours, and we copied some letters that were in Japanese and had them translated. You can see the translations if you like, but I wouldn't recommend it. It wouldn't help you at all. Just forget about her and concentrate on saving yourself."

Ryan looked crumpled, folded forward in the chair, his arms tightly folded across his stomach, Seymour continued, giving Ryan the opportunity of a little time to recover, "Personally I've given up on the whole idea of romantic love, women are such liars, such manipulators, they never tell you all the truth. I see a constant stream of them through this office. I believe that if it wasn't for sex, men and women would have the same relationship and mutual understanding as dogs and cats."

"Christ" was all Ryan said, the word coming out like a whisper. He looked ashen and withdrawn, Seymour wasn't sure if Ryan was listening to him at all, but Seymour continued in a quiet voice, almost talking to himself now,

"Do you know a painting called "The Meeting on the Turret Stairs" at all? It's in the National Gallery, but it's also a popular print. I have a copy; I keep it on my bedroom wall. A Norman Knight in full chain mail armour kissing the hand of a beautiful young woman in a long blue velvet dress on the stairway of a castle. All very sweet and romantic. But that's just the first impression. Then you start to look carefully at what's going on in this picture, you see she is turned away, he is kissing her arm and you start to think, just what is this, why is she turning away, is she already thinking of another meeting she has planned, is this poor fool saying goodbye before going out to get himself killed defending her honour? Like I say, I keep it on my bedroom wall. Everyone who sees it thinks that after all, I am a romantic. But it helps me if I get foolish notions. At least, it helps most of the time. I have a long and well proven track record of finding troublesome women for myself. We are all the architects of our own misfortunes on that front."

He looked over at Ryan, and continued talking for want of something better, sure that this was a private dialogue with himself, just making background while Tom Ryan tried to come to terms with the loss of Kara,

"You know, sitting in this chair, I see most of life unfolded in front of me, in all its blackness. It seems to me that most of the problems come from people living life through their wishes, whether it's business relationships or love affairs. It's reality that's the problem. Like we were never meant to be here in this reality, can't take it, don't have the equipment for it. Like we should have been on another planet where things work differently. So we wish. And that's where the problems come in. That's where I come in, come to think of it. A seeker of reality, the one they all pour out their troubles to. Looking for a magic solution, but there is no magic solution. No magic solution at all, not for any of us. Just life screwed up by our wishes. Perhaps we should all stop wishing, but then, maybe life would be entirely unbearable, because isn't reality unbearable for most people? So they do the lottery and they keep wishing. That's the way it seems from what I see from here. So we all go on. Wishing for unreal things."

Ryan by now had gathered himself together a little, he was sitting up straight again, but he was still deathly pale and looking as though someone had hit him hard in the stomach and the wind had been knocked out of him. He replied as though he had not been listening to Seymour, his voice taut and husky,
"Staying dead costs money. I had taken funds out of my account to cover the Easter weekend, but that won't last very long, not if I keep staying in bed and breakfast guest-houses. And I can hardly start making withdrawals from my bank account or using credit cards."

"Well since your friends blew up your car in their attempt to kill you, I suppose you might as well have some compensation. O'Sullivan left me some cash which I think could be regarded as rightfully yours under the circumstances. I'll get it for you. It's enough to keep you going for a while. Maybe I'll have a further idea later to try to fund your resurrection or maybe I should say reincarnation. But first you need to re-adjust, you need some time, some very quiet time."

Seymour disappeared into the adjoining room and came back a little later with two bundles of cash,
"This is what O'Sullivan paid me to find you. There is enough here to help keep you out of the way for the time being. This whole thing has caused me a lot of problems and there are more coming over the hill at me between Fitzpatrick and his friends in the Special Branch and the FBI. I need you out of the way and staying dead. Maybe that way we can put an end to this for both you and me."

# Chapter 30

There was a sudden and treacherous Summer gale and the wind was screaming through the rigging and superstructure of the small trawler. She was a long way from her home port of Galway. An angry hiss of airborne white spray filled the air. The sea was mountainous and vicious green and it was cold and dangerous off the coast of Northern Spain as the old trawler pitched, rolled, creaked, shuddered and strained against the might of the breaking chaos of a sea which attempted to swallow it whole. The skipper radioed that they had engine trouble and urgently requested a tug to tow her into the nearest port, Bilbao.

After making port and tying up securely, McIntyre reported to the Harbour Police and explained they had been towed in by a tug and would now have to wait for a marine diesel engine part to be delivered. He reckoned it would take a few days, the old engine was obsolete now. No, they had no fish on board. The Harbour Police said they would come down and inspect the trawler in a couple of hours. McIntyre assured them this was OK, no problem; the two crewmen would be on board if he wasn't, he was going for a drink with the Mate. The two officials glanced at this new Mate who looked so ill, but then smiled at McIntyre, McIntryre's drinking was notorious, even in Bilbao.

So far so good. All the formalities completed, McIntyre set off with Kelly to meet their Basque contact in one of the Harbour bars. The sea journey had taken it's toll on Kelly, but McIntyre thought he'd be OK, just put some hot whiskey into him in a warm pub.

As they walked on, he tried one last time,
"For the love of God Kelly, would you not think of going back now? What good can it do?"

"I've come a long way from the early days in Derry after I became involved in '69. Do you remember the radio call from Radio Free Derry, begging for help that never came, when we were left defenceless against the armed B-Specials. Nothing was done, there was no response, except for the few. The ones like Tom Ryan who came up to us. Well since then I've surely been responsible for a lot and no doubt I'll burn in hell for my trouble, but there are times when you have to do something to put things right, reach back and try to redress the past. Just think of all that has happened as a consequence of this bastard, all because of his selfishness."

McIntyre replied,
"I knew and admired Tom Ryan too. I knew him from the Fifties, when we were both youngsters, before he was shot and jailed, before your time. It grieves me, what happened. But this won't bring Tom Ryan back."

"For me, the fact that Ryan is dead is enough. And that bastard Prendergast knew right well what and who he was dealing with after Maguire's robbery at the Castleglen meat plant. And it's not as though he was short of money, as the manager he had more than enough both over and under the table. Just think of the consequences that flowed from Prendergast taking the cash, opportunistically moving in on our robbery. Well there's nothing else we can do now to try to put matters right, except this, so let's get on with it. I want to see some kind of justice done."

McIntyre said nothing, but Kelly had changed as a result of Ryan's death. Even if this job had to be done, it could have been delegated or even contracted out. This had become personal, had eaten away at Kelly, stirred up something irrational in him. McIntyre knew that Kelly had been sickened by the Army Council decision to execute Tom Ryan, knowing all the time it was wrong, being made a part of the decision, powerless to change it. Now they all knew it had been the wrong decision, too late. McIntyre and everyone else close to Kelly in the IRA, knew that Kelly had always played the game like a game of chess. Move and counter move. Trying to out-think the enemy, find new ways of inflicting damage, new defensive strategies, always seeking to optimise the limited military resources available to him against the greater resources of the enemy. He was now behaving differently, differently from all the years of war, the cold, deadly game he had resourcefully mastered. Putting himself at risk like this was crazy. He wondered if perhaps Kelly had had enough of the killing, now wanted peace, that this was some kind of final action for him, some kind of completion with the past. But McIntyre realized there was no going back now, Kelly would not be moved, was resolute and any further attempts by him to change Kelly's mind would be taken as hostile, disloyal.

It was just a small favour from the Basques, to drive the two of them into Portugal and then bring them back. And provide the two handguns. The Basque Separatists would get a favour in return. Those fighting in dirty wars needed to help each other when they could.

It took them the rest of that day and most of the next to drive across Spain and into Southern Portugal. On the long car journey, they talked about football mainly. No politics. No talk of armed actions, bombings or the like. Each knew all about that, there was no point in talking about it. The Basques and the Irish each knew enough about their own particular problems, each had already spent long enough talking about it in their own lives. There was nothing new to be said.

The Basque was younger than the two Irishmen, mid-thirties, but he had the same look about him. Someone who had been seasoned in violence, took a fatalistic view of life's prospects, had become familiar with death. He had looked death in the face and he too had become accustomed to living on the edge of society and had become immune to life's uncertain and unkind expectations. These men understood each other. There was an easy relaxed atmosphere in the car. Three men comfortable with each other. Knowing what they were about and accepting it as normal, necessary. Resigned to the reality of how things were.

The location was remote, but they had little trouble finding the sprawling farm with the re-construction work in progress. Local builders bringing the big old farmhouse up to modern standards for the Irishman who had recently bought it for his early retirement. The locals thought it was nice to be able to retire so early, he was still a relatively young man, maybe forty, forty-five. Prendergast had told them that his wife and family would join him later in the Summer, as soon as most of the work was completed on the house. Yes, everyone knew it was going to be really beautiful when he had it finished. The local builders and tradesmen were delighted with the work and paying cash ensured the work was done quickly and he had their full attention.

The three men waited in the car, tucked away in the cover of a group of trees beside the track as the evening light faded. They saw the last of the builder's trucks pull out, dust billowing as it drove down the track. Then they drove up and through the entrance gateway, two large wrought iron gates at the side, waiting to be painted and hung. The driver turned the car to face back down the driveway. The lights were on in the house now as Kelly got out of the car. McIntyre also got out and stood by the car, arms leaning on top of the car roof, his head resting on his folded arms, gazing back towards the house. The Basque driver stayed inside the car, ready to drive out again.

The front door of the house wasn't locked, Kelly just walked straight in, then walked easily and silently through the house following the direction of the sound of music coming from the radio. Kelly found him in the kitchen, busily arranging his evening meal on the old farmhouse table. He looked up in surprise, startled to find Kelly standing there.

*     *     *

McIntyre waited, looking back at the house, occasionally scanning the surrounding area and the driveway, listening, making sure nothing moved. The air was warm and sweet, everything was peaceful. After about ten minutes, Kelly came out, his jacket off, his shirt covered in blood, holding a towel to his shoulder,

"Are you OK, what happened?"

"Yes, just about. Fortunately the strap on the shoulder holster saved me, the bastard went mad and came at me with a bread knife."

"Do you want me to go in?"

"No, I took care of it. He didn't know how to use a knife." As he said it, the vision of Prendergast's face came back to Kelly's mind, the contorted face up against his own. The knife had come down at him, glancing off Kelly's shoulder as he first turned away, before Kelly caught Prendergast's forearm and broke his hold on the knife. Then Kelly had spun close in and fast, turning back to face Prendergast who was unbalanced and leaning forward and forced the bread-knife up with both hands, the blade going fast up through the lower jaw, then fully inserted into the head driving it back, the body now quivering like a fish just caught, Prendergast's groin obscenely thrusting against his own, the warm fresh blood running like a dark river and flowing down all over Kelly's upraised joined hands and down his arms and soaking into his shirt, like some awful ritualistic slaughter.

"He said one odd thing though before he went mad with the knife and tried to take me out. He said that two men had visited him a couple of weeks ago and demanded the funds he had stolen, brought him down to the local bank and had him withdraw the lot. I told the stupid bastard I didn't believe him since no one else knew about him and that I was here to collect. Then he came at me with the knife."

"Aye, that's an odd story alright."

The car drove on into the night. There was no further conversation for a while, only the driver was aware of the silence as McIntyre and Kelly each entered a private world created by their own thoughts. But such silences were familiar to the Basque in the aftermath, the period of anticlimax following an action and he just drove steadily on, pushing a music tape into the car player. The Basque was the only one who heard the mellow tones of Julio Iglesias.

Kelly started to reflect on the pent up anger and frustration that had been so violently released from him in killing Prendergast. The convoluted nature of the struggle he had devoted his life to, the problems of containing it in some ordered fashion, listening to the denunciations of the liberal commentators, the revisionist historians, the pathetic Southern Politicians, so conveniently removed from the situation on the ground, the dirty tricks of the British. The hard won cease-fire was being taken for granted, thrown back in their faces. Taken as a right, as though the IRA had been defeated. The politicians stood back and delivered nothing.

In terms of what he had directly done in his life and what

he was responsible for in the campaign of terror he had supervised, Prendergast was only a minor player in the larger events of Kelly's life. Yet it had been here and now that the dam had broken, the whole eruption of uncontrollable emotion shocking him by the depths and secret unacknowledged places from which it came. His whole body started to shiver.

McIntyre wondered what had happened to this man beside him, Kelly who played the game like chess. Cold and calculated, taking the losses and the gains experienced in the field of war with apparent equanimity. Something had changed, the ground on which Kelly had so firmly stood had moved. To McIntyre, this whole escapade was madness, a crazy risk taken for no sensible objective. His thoughts turned to Seymour. Seymour who knew more of the story than anyone else. For some reason, Kevin Ryan came into his mind, then left again. McIntyre knew where Kevin Ryan was, that he had been working on the new computer project for the IRA for the last two months. There was only one other player. Tom Ryan came into his mind, seemingly from nowhere. He started to rub his forehead which insisted on folding itself into concertina-like furrows, and he took a sideways look across at Kelly. Sweet Jesus, he thought, but he said nothing and looked away. His brain was befuddled by the enormity of the ludicrous prospect that confronted him, confoundedly insisting on holding itself up to him. He was overcome with the need for a drink and the desire to be alone. But the car drove on relentlessly, in the rush to get Kelly to a safe doctor.

# Epilogue

On Friday, February 9, 1996, an IRA active service unit bombed Canary Wharf in London, inflicting death, many casualties and massive destruction. The miraculous interlude of peace had lasted just eighteen months and the cease-fire was over. A transient dream of peace had died and was lost to the consuming spiral of evils, large and small, evils of commission and omission, a shedding of humanity, of empathy, of human warmth, of human love in the obscenity of war.

\*　　\*　　\*

Spring came in 1996, as always, bringing clouds of cherry blossom and then sweeps of yellow daffodils and Easter time again, the season of resurrection and renewed hope after the natural death of winter in the Northern Hemisphere, after the cold.

On Good Friday, April 14, 1996 at 10pm the phone rang in California and Ellen answered, and he heard her say,
"It's for you Jim, he just said you wouldn't know who it was, the line is very bad, it might be a call on a cell phone."

And as Tom Ryan waited alone and unsure, remembered

words came back, seemingly taunting him down the empty, near silent phone connection, part of the dispassionate electronic network which disinterestedly maintained it's existence, impervious in it's ability to bring good or bad news, a kind of permanent reprimand by being there, always offering the chance to connect him to the world. Thoughts echoed across the void of his mind, making sharp painful collisions in their unbidden journeys,

*So how is it now*
*Now that it's over*
*And why does it hurt so*
*Now that you're free*

*So when will it be better*
*Is it possible at all*
*When you can still remember*
*Can still recall*

*The vision of beauty, the touch of her hand*
*The smile, the voice, the loss of control*
*The love in the night*
*The awakening at dawn*

## Coming soon from John Devlin:

Four men meet in a spacious office, overlooking the East River. The oldest is an investment lawyer, the youngest an Irish businessman. They are both seated, as is a tall, thin man in a dark elegant business suit. But he sits a little removed from them. His sharp, angular features are looking across at the fourth man who is standing, staring, but not at the others. He has been walking back and forth behind a long bank of computer screens, stopping repeatedly as he checks the streaming stock prices. His attention is seemingly divided between the meeting and his usual worries as head of the brokerage firm. He and the other men in the room are gamblers, for this is the essential nature of the market and the funding of hi-tech business in the fast lane. But after this meeting concludes and they put their plans into effect, the lives of all of them will be frighteningly changed. It's a dangerous business with no turning back when you accept *"The Devil's Money"* .....

E-Mail your comments to words@aabspec.com and obtain up-dated information on the work of John Devlin.